P9-CED-081

"I don't need lunch," Kate managed

Richard Blair shook his head. "Don't they teach you anything in Australian medical schools?" he demanded. "Like the first rule of elementary psychology? Initial treatment of emotional crisis is always food. It's impossible to work oneself up to hysterics while one is eating a round of toasted cheese sandwiches and drinking cappuccino with three teaspoons of sugar."

He ushered Kate's unresisting body through the door. "Lunch, Dr. Harris!"

Marion Lennox has had a variety of careers, including medical receptionist, computer programmer and teacher. Married, with two young children, she now lives in rural Victoria, Australia. Her wish for an occupation that would allow her to remain at home with her children and her dog, led her to begin writing, and she has now published several romances with medical backgrounds.

A LOVING LEGACY
Marion Lennox

Harlequin Books

TORONTO • NEW YORK • LONDON
AMSTERDAM • PARIS • SYDNEY • HAMBURG
STOCKHOLM • ATHENS • TOKYO • MILAN
MADRID • WARSAW • BUDAPEST • AUCKLAND

If you purchased this book without a cover you should be aware
that this book is stolen property. It was reported as "unsold and
destroyed" to the publisher, and neither the author nor the
publisher has received any payment for this "stripped book."

ISBN 0-373-17219-2

A LOVING LEGACY

Copyright © 1994 by Marion Lennox.

First North American Publication 1995.

All rights reserved. Except for use in any review, the reproduction or
utilization of this work in whole or in part in any form by any electronic,
mechanical or other means, now known or hereafter invented, including
xerography, photocopying and recording, or in any information storage
or retrieval system, is forbidden without the written permission of the
publisher, Harlequin Enterprises Limited, 225 Duncan Mill Road,
Don Mills, Ontario, Canada M3B 3K9.

All characters in this book have no existence outside the imagination of
the author and have no relation whatsoever to anyone bearing the same
name or names. They are not even distantly inspired by any individual
known or unknown to the author, and all incidents are pure invention.

This edition published by arrangement with Harlequin Enterprises B.V.

® and TM are trademarks of the publisher. Trademarks indicated with
® are registered in the United States Patent and Trademark Office, the
Canadian Trade Marks Office and in other countries.

Printed in U.S.A.

CHAPTER ONE

KATE knew Betsy was due to die, but Betsy could have chosen a more timely death. At midnight, on a little-used track miles from the nearest house, was hardly ideal. To make matters worse, rain was coming down in buckets. Kate climbed from the driver's seat, walked to the front of the car and swore. Then she burst into tears.

Neither action helped. Her car was dead. From under the rusty bonnet came the unmistakable stench of burning rubber, and the rain falling on the hot metal was hissing back as steam.

By the time the Mercedes came up behind her, Kate was almost past noticing. The rain had soaked her to the skin, making her jeans and windcheater cling dankly to her slight body. Her dark chestnut curls were hanging in dripping tendrils across her face and rivulets of water were running down her pale cheeks. The big silver Mercedes rounded the bend and swerved to a skidding halt, its headlights slashing through the rain to light both Kate and her decrepit car.

'What the hell. . .?' The driver emerged swiftly from his car. He was tall and fair, and his voice was deeply resonant. Kate's car was blocking the road on a blind bend, and his voice held the edge of shock. Then, as shock faded, he crossed to where Kate was standing. She really did look a bedraggled waif.

'Need a hand, then, lady?' The alarm in the stranger's voice was replaced by amusement.

Kate flushed. She was bone-weary, struggling to keep tears at bay, and the last thing she wanted was an arrogant male playing knight in shining armour for his own entertainment. She had no choice, though, but to accept the role of helpless female. The life of three-year-old Tracy could well depend on it.

'My car's broken down,' she managed.

'Really? I thought you might have just stopped here to admire the view.' The laughter deepened. 'Sure it hasn't just run out of petrol?'

'I'm sure.' Kate's green eyes flashed anger. She pushed a sodden wisp of hair out of her eyes and dug her hands in her pockets. 'It's overheated.'

Then, as if to prove her point, her ancient car proceeded to demonstrate. The hissing of steam suddenly built, there was a dull thud and the engine erupted in a ball of fire.

Her bag. . . Her bag was still in the car. Kate drew in her breath in horror and moved forward. The stranger made a grab towards her, gripping her arm.

'Don't be stupid——'

He wasn't fast enough. Kate wrenched her arm from his grasp and kept going. She couldn't let her bag burn. It held everything she needed. Her fingers gripped the car door-handle, already hot to touch, and she hauled the rear door open. As she reached in to grip the battered leather case lying on the seat, the stranger grabbed her from behind and unceremoniously hauled her from the car.

The case came too. The man was strong, far too strong for Kate to fight, and strong enough to haul the combined weight of Kate and her heavy case back from the burning car. Then, as she was thrown heavily to the sodden roadside turf, the stranger's body came down to shield her and the car erupted in a sheet of flames.

For a long moment Kate lay still. All the breath had been knocked out of her, and the stranger's weight was still on her, pressing her down. The heat of the car flickered around them, searingly hot.

Still Kate's fingers clutched her case. Finally, as the

flames died down, the stranger shifted and moved back from her body. He stood and stared down at the girl crouched at his feet. Even in the near dark, Kate could see his anger.

'What the hell do you have in that case?' he said savagely. The laughter had disappeared entirely from his voice. 'You realise you nearly got us both killed?'

'I'm. . .' Kate rose stiffly to a sitting position, the moisture from the ground soaking through her clothes. 'I'm sorry. . .

'It had better be diamonds.' From the sound of the man's voice Kate knew he'd been badly rattled. 'Come to think of it, I don't think diamonds are worth it.' He gave a harsh laugh and rose to stare at the burning wreck. 'Don't tell me,' he said bitterly. 'Your favourite cocktail dress?'

'It's a medical bag,' Kate said quietly. 'I need it. . .'

'A medical bag. . .'

'Yes.' Kate stared bleakly at what was left of her car and then turned to the man beside her. He was so big. Big and fair and angry. . . 'Could you drive me to the nearest farm, please?' she said.

'Is that where you live?'

'N-no. But the Robertsons will drive me. . .'

'Drive you where?' The man's voice was still harsh and cold.

'I'm a doctor,' Kate told him, rising to her feet. 'I'm on an urgent call. Tracy Cameron. . .'

'A doctor!' It was an exclamation of disbelief.

Kate managed a faint laugh. 'I know I'm not your common image of a general practitioner,' she said. 'But I am a doctor, and the Cameron child sounds sick. I have to go.'

'I don't believe it.' The stranger's voice was flat with incredulity.

'It's true.' Kate drew herself up. 'Doctors don't have to be middle-aged and male, you know.'

Silence. The man's face was blank with incomprehension. He seemed stunned.

'Please,' Kate said softly. 'Please. . . If I don't go Tracy might die.'

'What's wrong with her?' The stranger's words were forced and hard, as if acceptance had been difficult.

'I think—I hope—that she just has croup.' Kate turned to meet his dark eyes full-on. He was in his thirties, she thought, and so large! Kate was tall, but this man made her feel diminutive. His penetrating eyes looked straight through her. 'Will you take me?' Her voice faltered. 'Just as far as the Robertsons'. They'll take me on.'

For a long moment there was silence. The man was staring down at her and his dark eyes still held anger. And something else. It was as if he didn't want to accept what she was telling him.

Maybe he was another of the males who thought women doctors were an anathema, Kate thought bitterly. If he refused to take her. . .

'Get in.' The man was striding across to fling open the passenger door of the Mercedes. Kate gaped.

'You. . . You'll take me to the Robertsons?'

'I'll take you to your patient,' he growled. 'Let's go.'

It was a ten-minute drive to the Cameron farm. By the time they reached it, the warmth of the car had cured Kate's shivering. She was still shocked and exhausted, however, and gave the man beside her curt directions with no embellishments. He also showed no inclination to talk.

Kate's fingers where she had touched the hot doorhandle were stinging painfully. She looked down at them in the dim light. They were already starting to blister. She looked up and caught the edge of the stranger's glance.

'They'll need attention or they'll get infected,' he said roughly.

Kate flushed. It seemed he really hadn't taken her medicine seriously.

'I know,' she told him.

The small farmhouse was lit up as if waiting. The sleek Mercedes turned into the gate and half a dozen dogs greeted them with enough noise to waken the dead. There was no need for their warning. John Cameron emerged from the house before the car had pulled up and Kate was almost dragged from the car. The stranger beside Kate was ignored. John Cameron wanted Kate, and he wanted her desperately.

'She's worse.' The farmer's voice was a plea. 'She doesn't even seem to have the strength to cough. And she's blue. . .'

Kate glanced over at the driver of the car, but the farmer had seized her hand, pulling her relentlessly out of the car and towards the house. At the door, despite the pressure of the farmer's hand, Kate stopped and looked back. The stranger was standing beside the car. His face was expressionless.

'Thank you,' Kate managed. 'M-my case?'

'I'll bring it in,' the stranger said coldly. 'Go on.'

Kate had no choice. The pressure on her hand increased and she was dragged inside. The stranger was left standing by the car, watching her.

The first thing that hit Kate was the silence. She had been called because Tracy Cameron was suffering with croup. On the phone Kate had been hardly able to hear the terrified mother for the harsh, barking cough accompanying croup's stridor. Now. . . Kate followed the farmer with a sinking heart, knowing what she would find.

The farmer led Kate through to a bedroom at the rear of the house. As he swung open the door Kate finally heard the child. The cough had given way to a rasping gasp for breath. The stridor was unmistakable.

It was weak, as though the child was losing the fight to keep breathing.

The child's pallor confirmed Kate's fears. Mrs Cameron was seated on the bed, the little girl cradled in her arms. The child was just three, with a pinched, elfin face and eyes that were huge for her body. The little one's terror was palpable as she fought for breath. Kate looked swiftly around the bedroom.

'Didn't I tell you to keep her in steam?'

'We ran out of hot water.'

'Well, get some more.' Kate's tone was brusque, cutting through the parents' terror. There was no time for gentle reassurance. Swiftly she lifted the little girl from her mother's arms and carried her through to the kitchen. 'Have you an electric frying-pan?'

'Yes. . .' The father had kept up with her. 'I. . . It's in the cupboard.'

'Fill it with water and turn it on.' Kate's memories of her burnt-out car and the tall, fair stranger were pushed aside as the urgency of the little girl's plight took hold. For now, all Kate had room for was her medicine. 'I want every pot in the house filled with water and on the stove, with the stove stoked up to full blast.'

As the farmer turned to carry out Kate's instructions the mother caught up with them. She looked dazed and shocked, and at the point where she was expecting the worst.

'I want an old blanket, or big towels,' Kate told her. And then, as the woman started to weep, Kate's voice hardened. 'I need them now,' she said harshly. 'You can cry afterwards, but not now. And I need my case. . .'

The woman gulped, ran her hand across her tear-stained cheek and turned away. As she did, the driver of the Mercedes entered the room and laid Kate's case on the table. After one swift look at the child in Kate's arms, he lifted the lid and bent to inspect the contents.

'Nebuliser?'

Kate stared, but then caught herself. 'Yes,' she said brusquely. 'Underneath the dressing. . .'

The man had seen it. Swiftly he pulled it from the case and hooked it to a mask. Kate was checking her tiny patient's airway. As she finished, the mask was put into her hand.

'Adrenalin?' the man asked.

'It should be there.' Who on earth was this man? With his bulky home-knit jumper, his moleskin trousers and elastic-sided boots and his tanned, open face, Kate had taken him for a farmer. What was a farmer doing with the medical knowledge this man so obviously possessed? She shrugged inwardly. There was no time for questions.

'No wonder the case was so heavy.' The stranger handed her the adrenalin.

'Yes,' Kate said shortly, her attention swinging back to the little girl in her arms. The option of a breathing tube was being weighed in her mind.

'Try the adrenalin first,' the stranger advised, as though guessing her thoughts. 'You have time.'

'How do you. . .?'

'Not much time. You organise the nebuliser,' the man told her. 'I'll set up a tent.'

Within minutes the stranger had organised a make-shift steam tent, hooking blankets and towels over chairs propped on the kitchen table. Inside, the frying-pan boiled its load of hot water. As the last blanket was adjusted over her head, Kate glanced across at the parents.

'Now for the soggy part.' She forced a smile as she looked up at the mother. 'You can cry now if you like,' she said softly. 'But I wouldn't. There's no need.' She looked hesitatingly up at the stranger, a hundred questions crowding into her head, but the child whimpered in her arms and struggled feebly against the mask. Kate turned back to her. There would be time for questions when the little girl was safe.

The stranger smiled down at her, as if he knew her queries and understood her silence. The smile made Kate catch her breath. It lit his face, causing the deep lines around his eyes to crease with laughter. Then the blanket descended. The memory of the smile stayed with her as Kate and the little girl were placed in soggy isolation.

It was fifteen minutes before Kate could see any improvement. Kate stayed under the blanket with the child, holding her as close to the steam as she dared. The blanket above her was dripping with moisture, and sweat and condensation had soaked both Kate and her little patient, but gradually the awful blue had faded.

As the adrenalin in the pump finished, Kate removed the mask. The coughing started again—the rasping bark that Kate had heard on the phone. At least the cough meant Tracy was regaining her strength. As she did, though, the child's panic deepened.

Kate concentrated on keeping the child calm, speaking soothingly and softly, humming tiny crooning nothings that calmed the fear away from the little face. Kate had considered briefly having the mother hold the child but one look at Dorothy Cameron had been enough to change her mind. The woman's face reflected terror and it would be impossible not to communicate that to an already desperately frightened child.

Outside the blanket she could hear the parents talking in soft murmurs as a backdrop to her own humming, and a couple of times she heard the stranger speaking quietly. Who was he? She was sure she knew the locals. Therefore he must have come from outside the valley. What on earth was he doing here?

And why is it important to know? she asked herself. It wasn't, she responded severely. It was just that. . .

Just that what? In the gloomy humidity of the tent she shook her head in disgust at herself. It was just that he had made such an impression on her, she acknowledged. And why? Just because the man had a smile which made her heart lurch. . .

She bent over her little patient, rechecking her pulse for the hundredth time. She was winning the fight here, she knew, and that had to be all that mattered. There would be time for every other consideration later.

Finally, the harsh, barking cough ceased. The breathing eased to almost normal. As the child fell into an exhausted sleep, Kate lifted the blanket away.

The room was almost as full of steam as the makeshift tent, with half a dozen pots boiling fiercely on the stove. It was unbearably hot. Through the fog, Kate smiled at the parents, still standing at attention over the stove.

She cast an involuntary glance around for the stranger. He was gone. Kate was aware of a sharp stab of disappointment. Giving an inward shrug of her shoulders, she motioned to the sleeping child and Dorothy Cameron came forward.

'She'll get through,' she reassured the frightened woman. 'I'm afraid you're going to have to keep this steam up until morning, though. If you made up a bed for her in here, she'll sleep through, and it's the best thing for her.'

'She doesn't. . . She doesn't need to go to hospital?' the woman stammered.

Kate considered, wishing for the thousandth time that the valley had its own hospital. Normally a child this ill should be monitored by trained medical staff, but the nearest hospital was two hours' drive away. A two-hour drive without steam could well prove fatal.

'I think she'll be safe where she is. If you can put me up for the night, I'll stay.'

'You haven't a choice,' the farmer smiled. 'You've been deserted. Your friend waited to see that things

were OK. When Tracy's cough eased he said he'd leave
you to it. We told him we'd take you home.'

Kate frowned. 'He's not my friend,' she said shortly.
'My car broke down and he gave me a lift. Did he tell
you who he was?'

'No.' The farmer was standing aside to let her pass
from the kitchen. Clearly he was anxious to get back to
his bed now the drama had passed. Behind him, his
wife was settling the sleeping little girl on to a sofa in
the corner of the kitchen. 'I'll show you where you can
sleep.'

Kate allowed herself to be ushered out. She was
aware that she was close to total exhaustion herself. A
glance at her watch showed her that it was three in the
morning. She had patients booked for morning surgery
at nine, and there was now the added difficulty of no
car. She put a weary hand to her eyes and tried to blot
out the complications crowding in on her. For now, all
that mattered was sleep.

The household stirred early. From semi-consciousness
Kate heard the farmer rise just before dawn to go and
bring in the cows. This was dairy country, and the
Camerons had a small herd. No matter what happened
to the family, the cows had to be milked twice a day.

By six-thirty, the older Cameron children were stir-
ring, and inquisitive faces were peeping around her
door. Kate sighed, dredged up a smile for the curious
faces and pulled off her covers. She pulled on her jeans
and windcheater, still damp from the night before, and
emerged to face another day.

Just after eight the farmer drove her home. Kate's
little patient had woken and seemed to be fine, with
nothing worse wrong with her but a head cold. The
drama of the night before might never have happened.

'She may have a recurrence over the next couple of
nights,' Kate warned. 'You know what to do now,

though, and I'd be surprised if it gets as bad again. If I were you I'd let her sleep in the kitchen until her cold clears, and leave a pot of water simmering on the stove.'

'We'll do that,' Mrs Cameron promised. She took Kate's hands and gripped them. 'Thank you, Kate.'

The farmer drove her slowly down through the valley, his noisy old truck shattering the early morning calm of the countryside. August in the south-east corner of Australia meant country which was green and lush. The huge gums along the roadside still dripped from the rainfall of the night before.

The small town of Corrook lay at the lowest point of the valley, before the road snaked uphill again to Kate's home. The town was deserted at this time of the morning, with the single row of shops locked and lifeless.

The farmer was uncommunicative as they drove. He'd slept as little as Kate and, with his cows milked and Kate delivered home, he was looking forward to crawling back to his bed for a couple of hours.

Half his luck, Kate thought enviously, and then her uncharitable thoughts were driven from her head at the sight of the main street.

Corrook's main thoroughfare consisted of a dozen shops and a pub, so each building stood out. The last sizeable building was a supermarket. Nestled beside it was the small shop where Alf, the local pharmacist, dispensed drugs, advice and criticism of 'the lady doctor' in equal quantities. Finally there was the neat little building labelled, falsely now for two years, 'Doctor's Surgery'.

Outside this building, for those two years, had stood an imposing 'For Sale' sign. Every time Kate had come to town she had stared longingly at the little building. There was no way she could buy it, though, and Alf, just as certainly, wasn't going to lease it, especially, as

he put it bluntly, to 'some quack of a woman pretending
to play doctors'. They had achieved an impasse, with
Kate being forced to practise from her isolated farmhouse and Alf owning an unused doctor's surgery.

This morning the sign still stood. There was a change,
however. From one side to the other was plastered a
huge red notice. 'Sold'.

Kate gave an audible gasp, and the farmer was roused
from his contemplation of future sleep.

'Well, will you look at that! Alf's finally found a
buyer.'

Kate shook her head in disbelief. It was the end, she
thought tiredly. The last nail in the coffin of her lovely
dream. Somehow she had hoped against hope that one
day she would practise from that building.

'He's always said he'll only sell it to a doctor,' John
Cameron told her. 'And Alf's not one to change his
mind.'

Kate shook her head wearily. After her initial shock
it didn't matter. Her mind was dulled by fatigue and
hopelessness. The sale of the surgery seemed not to
concern her. In fact it might be a good thing if it had
been sold to a doctor. She could put her little farm on
the market and leave with a clear conscience. Without
a car she had no choice anyway. Her career in country
general practice was over.

CHAPTER TWO

KATE had twenty minutes to herself before morning surgery. She showered, changed into a serviceable skirt, blouse and her white coat and wandered back into her front room to wait for Mrs Quayle.

Bella Quayle acted as Kate's combined receptionist and mother hen. She had taken 'the lady doctor' under her wing when Kate arrived in the valley two years ago and had stood between her and the world ever since.

It seemed an age since Kate had arrived at Corrook. Her little farm had been bought on a whim, in the days when money was plentiful and Doug was spending with abandon. 'It'll be an investment,' he had told Kate, placing the deeds on the dinner-table one night. 'I took it in lieu of a debt. And because it's our wedding anniversary, my love, I've put it in your name.'

It was another of Doug's dubious deals. He had always been an ambitious accountant but the boom of the Eighties had gone to his head. Nothing Kate could say seemed to make any difference to his need to place them deeper and deeper into debt.

The derelict farm was the only thing in Kate's name. Intent on building up her tiny city practice, immersed in the medicine she loved, she had left her financial affairs in Doug's hands. After all, he was an accountant and her husband. She had been with Doug since her late teens and she trusted him completely. As it happened, she was a fool to do so.

The surgery, her home, her car — everything — had been mortgaged to the hilt. Her security was based on her trust of her husband, and when Doug decided he had made one clever financial move too many and it

17

would be better for him to leave the country he had
repaid that trust by buying first-class air tickets for
himself and a woman 'friend' Kate hadn't known
existed. She had been left with an aching heart, bitter
memories and a mountain of bills it would take years to
clear.

If she had been like her husband, Kate would have
walked away from her husband's debts. Kate Harris,
however, had a conscience, and money was owed to
people she knew. To her horror she discovered that
even her parents had lent money to Doug. He had
persuaded them to mortgage their home to finance their
daughter's surgery—'Without telling Kate, of course,
because it would hurt her pride to know that I'm
asking.' Kate's surgery had been sold, but not for near
enough to redeem the mortgage, and her practice in the
city had ceased to exist.

The farm had been the last thing she had put on the
market. She had come down to Corrook one cold,
bleak weekend when life was at its worst, with the
intention of finding an agent to sell the house. Instead
she had met Tim Quayle, husband of Bella, estate
agent for Corrook and district.

'You're crazy to sell,' he told her bluntly. 'The rural
industry's in recession, same as everywhere else. You
won't get half what you paid for it. And besides. . .' he
eyed her shrewdly, and his eyes discovered more than
Kate knew she revealed '. . .Corrook's desperate for a
doctor. Come and live here. Mother!' he called into the
residence behind his shop front. 'Come and meet
Corrook's new GP.'

It had seemed crazy, but the alternative was a salar-
ied job and moving back home with her parents. She
couldn't bear it. Kate had been close to suffocating in
the sympathy of her family and friends, and the chance
to get away seemed heaven-sent.

But still there were bills to be paid. Her earnings

went straight to Doug's debtors, and without capital to set up a proper surgery or run a decent car it was impossible to go on. She had hoped to work her way clear, but it was as much as she could do to meet the interest repayments on the debts.

She would tell Bella this morning, Kate decided. This place, the tiny weather-board cottage and its surrounding few acres of neglected pasture could go on the market today.

Bella had to wait to be told. Two patients arrived before Kate's tardy receptionist and by the time Kate had a moment to talk there was a queue of six in the tiny sitting-room that served as a reception area.

'I've got some news,' Bella hissed as Kate emerged to receive the next patient's card.

'If it's about Alf's surgery being sold, then I know,' Kate said dully. She turned to an elderly lady seated near the door and summoned a smile.

'Come through, Mrs Breuhaut. I'm sorry I've kept you waiting.'

She had to apologise to every patient as the morning wore on. Each patient seemed to have difficult problems that required time, and they all wanted to talk about the sale of Alf's surgery.

By the time the reception area was cleared it was after two. Kate came out of her consulting-room to find Bella alone and gave a sigh of relief.

'Thank heaven for that.'

'You won't say that when you see your list of house calls,' Bella said darkly. 'And I know your car died last night. You can't keep anything to yourself for more than five minutes in this valley, especially if you leave a burnt car on the road. I rang Tim, and a couple of farmers will be up with tractors this afternoon to clear up the mess. Pete Symons — the local taxi driver — will take you on calls until it's fixed.'

Kate smiled gratefully. 'Thanks, Bella.' She sighed

and her eyes met the elderly woman's concerned look.
'You must have noticed that it's unfixable, though. I'm
afraid I can't go on.'

'No.' Bella looked down at her plump hands. 'I guess
not. Not with Alf selling the surgery.'

'To a doctor?'

'To a doctor,' Bella said. She sighed. 'Alf's been
dealing with this man for a month, it seems, without
letting anyone in the valley know. He's sold the surgery
and organised this doctor to rent the old Stevenson
farm down the road from here. Sly old coot, he is! He
needs Tim now, though. Seems this new doctor has also
bought the old hospital up the back of the town and
wants the parcel of land at the back that's on Tim's
books—for a nursing-home wing later on, I gather.'
She looked up at Kate and tried not to look excited.
'He's reopening the entire hospital. Won't that be
something for the town?'

'It should be fantastic,' Kate said slowly. 'I just wish
it were me that was doing it.'

Bella was silent. Finally she reached down and
started packing up her basket. 'You'll go back to the
city?'

'I have to,' Kate said sadly. 'Even if I had the means
to buy another car, I can't compete with a doctor whose
surgery's in town.'

Bella nodded sadly. 'We'll miss you,' she said simply.
'You're a fine doctor, Katy Harris.'

'With no business head and a hopeless taste in
husbands,' Kate finished bitterly. 'But thanks, Bella.'
Then her eyes went to the window as she heard a car
pulling into the yard. Another patient?

It wasn't a local. The big silver Mercedes was unmistakable. The car door opened and there was no mistak-
ing the man who emerged. It was the stranger of the
night before.

Bella had picked up her basket and turned to leave.

Now she hesitated, torn between her desire to get home to her very late lunch or to stay and check out this interesting visitor. She looked uncertainly at Kate.

'You go,' Kate told her. 'Tim will be wondering where you are.' She smiled. 'And thanks, Bella.'

'You're not leaving today?' Bella's voice sounded horrified.

'Of course I'm not,' Kate reassured her. 'I have a fully booked week already. I'm going to have to find someone to hand over to before I walk out.'

She walked out to the veranda. Bella followed her, cast a curious glance at the man striding up the steps, then set her mind firmly on her lunch. The man nodded pleasantly to Bella and then stood and watched until Bella's little car motored off down the hill.

'That leaves you stranded, Dr Harris,' the stranger mocked gently. Walking slowly up the steps to where Kate stood on the veranda, he motioned to the empty car park.

'There's a taxi,' Kate said, her colour mounting. If anything this man seemed almost larger than the night before. He was superbly built, with a strong and muscled frame. His brown eyes looked down at her quizzically, shaded by his unruly mass of fair hair. Kate was five feet nine in bare feet and was unused to being looked down on. It was a strange feeling. Her colour deepened.

'You know my name,' she said stiffly.

'I've belatedly done my homework,' he smiled ruefully. He held out a large hand. 'Richard Blair.'

Kate didn't return the smile, nor did she lift her hand to receive his.

'Dr Blair, I gather.'

He was standing a foot from her on the veranda, looking down at the white-coated girl with the eyes that were too big for her face. Her deep chestnut hair accentuated the pallor of her face. Two crimson spots stained her cheeks as if she was mortified.

'Yes,' he said slowly.

'Why didn't you tell me?' Kate asked quietly.

Richard Blair sighed and dug his hands into his moleskins. He was wearing a checked, open-necked shirt. He didn't look like a doctor. He looked far too casual.

'I didn't know how,' he confessed. 'I appear to have made a major professional blunder.'

Kate looked up, surprised. 'What do you mean?'

'You think I'd have bought into this valley if I knew there was already a doctor here?' he demanded. 'Your local pharmacist informed me there wasn't a doctor within forty miles. I couldn't believe my luck.'

'So you bought the place on a whim?'

'Something like that,' he agreed. His eyes crinkled into a reluctant smile and he gazed out over the valley. The view from Kate's veranda was breathtaking, out over the farmland to the tiny township below. At the base of the gully the river snaked its way through the massive gums that grew along its banks, curving away out of sight. A flock of crimson rosellas had risen screeching from the gums and formed a fast-wheeling scarlet flash in the sky. There was no other sound except for the faint whisper of wind through the trees.

'I've been in England,' he said quietly. 'I was born here but my mother was English. When I was sixteen my dad died and she took me back to England. She wanted me to stay, but when she died homesickness got the better of me.' He shrugged. 'Australia's home, even after an absence of twelve years. On return I drove through Western Victoria, just remembering how much space this country had. I turned down a back road to Corrook and saw Alf's sign.' His eyes lit with a rueful smile. 'End of story.'

Alf's sign. 'DOCTOR'S SURGERY FOR SALE.'

The sign Kate had looked at every time she went to town. If Kate had been in Richard Blair's position she might have done the same thing. If. . .

'It's a bit different from an English practice,' Kate said slowly.

'It's what I want,' he told her. 'I've had enough of cities to last a lifetime.' His smile faded and he looked down at her. 'Enough of me. I'm here to talk about you.' He hesitated. 'What the hell made Alf tell me there was no doctor here?'

'I'm a woman,' Kate said shortly. She wished he'd stop looking at her. The deep brown eyes and the man's size were making her nervous. Nervous? Or was it something else? The concern behind those brown eyes was catching at something deep within. . .

'I've noticed you're a woman,' Dr Blair retorted drily. 'You haven't answered my question.'

'I have,' Kate said, and her voice was etched with fatigue. 'Alf Burrows thinks a woman's place is in the home, preferably barefoot and pregnant. A woman doctor, for Alf, is a contradiction in terms. I can be one or the other, but not both. He fills my prescriptions under duress and tells anyone who'll listen that it'd be wiser to take their flu or chicken pox forty miles for a consultation rather than see me.' She smiled ruefully. 'So I guess you were the answer to his prayers.'

The concern deepened in Richard Blair's eyes. He sighed and dug his hands further into his pockets. 'I've done my homework really well,' he said bitterly. 'I've read maps and census figures. I know the population this town supports and I know the potential practice figures. The only thing I didn't know was that the place already had a doctor.' He shrugged. 'I should have checked but I couldn't see a pharmacist lying about something so basic.'

Kate shrugged. There was no point in continuing with the conversation.

'He has what he's been working for now,' she said bitterly. She turned to go inside. 'I'll hand over my patient's cards to you. Today if you like. You might as well start now.'

He swung around, startled. 'What the hell do you mean by that?'

'Well, I can't keep practising in the valley,' Kate said harshly. 'Not with Dr Blair in a nice central doctor's surgery, complete with private hospital too, I hear.'

'So you'll just walk out and leave me to it?'

'I have no choice.'

Richard Blair met her angry eyes. His expression remained calm. 'Are you sure that's not just a cop-out?' he said quietly.

'What do you mean?'

Richard shrugged. 'It doesn't seem that your practice is exactly prospering,' he said wryly. 'In fact I'm starting to wonder whether I have the figures right. Does the town need a doctor? How can you be as impoverished as you seem? Or are you just too lousy to invest in decent rooms and a car that'll get you to patients when they need you?'

'That's right,' Kate said bitterly. 'I hoard my money under my bed.' She walked back inside.

For a moment Richard Blair hesitated and then he followed her in. Kate started pulling open filing drawers and removing files.

'Do you want these now? I have a list of five house calls for this afternoon and I'm darned if I'll spend my hoard under the mattress on a taxi. If you're Corrook's new doctor, you can do them, Dr Blair.'

Richard Blair leaned against the receptionist's desk and folded his arms.

'Bitter, aren't we, Dr Harris?'

'What do you think?' she threw at him. 'You walk in here and buy my livelihood from under me. . .'

'It's hardly your livelihood,' he said carefully. 'Dr Harris, I was acting on a misapprehension when I bought Alf's surgery, but it seems Alf is right. This valley needs a comprehensive medical service and you are not providing that.' His dark eyes met her angry green ones. 'For instance, let's assume your car had got you to the Camerons' last night. You still might have felt the need to spend the night. What happens if there's an emergency somewhere else? How are you contacted? You weren't carrying a mobile phone last night. Do you have one?'

'No.'

'Why not?'

'Because I can't afford one.' Kate's hold on her temper was slipping and mostly it was because she knew this man was right.

Richard walked over to the desk and picked up Bella's appointment book. He flicked back through the last pages and then looked up again at Kate.

'That's rubbish,' he said harshly. 'You've been fully booked for weeks. With the income from solo practice you must be able to afford the tools to ensure competent service.'

Kate snatched the book from his hands. 'How dare you?' she snapped. 'How dare you look at something that's none of your business?'

He looked at her and nodded. 'You're right. It's none of my business. But unfortunately I feel morally obliged to offer you a partnership, or at least an associateship. According to the figures, this district could support two of us, and if you run your two-bit outfit while I set up shop in the main street then business is going to be a bit lop-sided.'

'I don't want a partnership,' Kate snapped. 'I'm leaving.'

'Why?'

'Because I can't afford to stay.' Exhaustion and

tension were catching up with Kate and she was very close to tears. 'I can't afford to go into partnership with you and I can't afford to keep running a practice here. And you're right. I don't provide good service. I'm sure you'll provide much better. Now if you'll excuse me.' She thrust the patient files at Richard Blair. 'Here's your list of house calls. I wish you the best of luck.' She turned away, fighting to keep tears from her eyes.

She wasn't successful. Tears were slipping down regardless. The silence in the reception-room stretched on and on.

Damn him. Why wouldn't he go? All Kate wanted was to be left alone to wallow in her misery. Then Richard's hand was on her shoulder and she was being pulled around to face him.

'My initial impression was right, wasn't it?' he asked, and his voice had softened. The concern was back in his eyes. 'You're exhausted.'

'I am not exhausted,' Kate flung at him, and her voice caught on a sob. 'I'm just angry.'

'Exhausted and angry,' he said equably. He glanced at his watch. 'Have you had lunch?'

'No. And I don't want any.' Kate's voice was childish with frustration and she bit her lip, turning her face from his careful scrutiny.

Richard glanced down at the files in his hands and then again at the tear-drenched face of the girl before him.

'Lunch,' he said firmly. 'Let's see if the Corrook café runs to take-away sandwiches and coffee.'

'I don't need lunch,' Kate managed.

Richard Blair shook his head. 'Don't they teach you anything in Australian medical schools?' he demanded. 'Like the first rule of elementary psychology? Initial treatment of emotional crises is always food. It's impossible to work oneself up to hysterics while one is eating a round of toasted cheese sandwiches and drinking cappuccino with three teaspoons of sugar.' He put a hand around Kate's shoulders and ushered her unresisting body through the door. 'Lunch, Dr Harris!'

CHAPTER THREE

As FAR as elementary psychology went, Dr Blair's rule worked wonders. By the time Kate had consumed two rounds of sandwiches and three cups of coffee she was almost under control. She leaned back on the luxurious upholstery of Richard's car and sipped her final cup, letting the sweetness of her cappuccino do its job.

Richard hadn't talked. He had the radio on, and soft, crooning tunes played one after another, filling any awkward silence. Richard ate and listened, seemingly intent on anything but the girl beside him.

As he finished his coffee he took Kate's files and studied them. When she put her own cup down he placed the files on the back seat and raised his eyebrows.

'Another?' They were sitting outside the café.

Kate dredged up a smile. 'No, thank you,' she told him. 'Three is quite enough. Mrs Cliff—the lady who owns the café—must think we're crazy. Sitting outside like this. . .'

'I told her we had confidential business matters to discuss,' Richard Blair said. 'Mrs Cliff understands perfectly.'

Kate choked on a reluctant giggle. 'She'll be agog,' she told him. 'Two doctors sitting in the town's main street drinking coffee from polystyrene mugs.' She put a hand to her face. 'And I'll bet she's seen from there that I've been crying. Your reputation might be lost before you've begun, Dr Blair.'

Richard smiled, encouraging the first trace of laughter he had seen in the girl beside him. 'Maybe I'll just have to marry you and be done with it.'

Kate's smile faltered and she looked away. 'It's not as bad as that,' she said quietly.

He stared at her, as if trying to read her emotion from her averted head. Finally he sighed and turned on the ignition.

'We've had our break,' he said firmly. 'Work, Dr Harris.' He motioned to the files on the back seat. 'Give me directions.'

'To where?' she asked blankly.

'In case you've forgotten your house calls, I haven't,' he reminded her. 'I've been reading your files. Where do we go first? Mr King's legs need checking, and it's time for Miss Mavis Souter's monthly visit. Or maybe the Grunter twins. . .'

Kate bit her lip. 'They're your patients,' she said slowly.

'I'm not taking them on without an introduction,' Richard said gravely. He nosed the big car carefully out into the street. 'Let's go.'

It was less difficult than Kate had imagined. Richard Blair fell silent as they approached the ramshackle cottage that was their first patient's home and left the talking to Kate.

'This is Dr Blair.' Kate introduced her companion to Herbert King, their first patient for the afternoon.

The old man looked Richard over critically and held out his hand. He had shuffled painfully to the door to let them in and was obviously hurting. 'G'day, Doc,' he said gruffly. 'I heard we had a new'n.' He shot an appraising look at Kate. 'Word is, though, he's competition — not a partner. Alf Burrows has been boasting all over town that he's cooked your goose.'

Richard smiled and shook his head. 'I couldn't compete with your Dr Harris,' he told the old man.

The old man stared at him through bushy eyebrows

and gave a snort. 'You wouldn't want to,' he said grimly. 'She's a good girl, Katy Harris.'

Kate flushed and put a hand under the old man's elbow. 'Let's get you back to bed,' she said gently.

Bert pulled his arm away roughly, his pride hurt. 'I can manage.'

'I know you can,' Kate said, tucking her arm again through his. 'I'm just acting possessive in case Dr Blair gets any ideas.'

The old man gave a cackle of delighted laughter and his wrinkled hand closed on Kate's. 'There's no competition at all,' he flung over his shoulder to Richard. 'Katy Harris is the best GP Corrook's ever had.'

'Since there's only ever been old Doc Macguire who hit the bottle, and me, that's hardly something to boast about.' Kate was guiding the old man carefully back to bed. He was frail and bent, and his steps were very unsure. Bert King should hardly be at home by himself, but the old man was putting up a determined fight to stay out of institutions.

With Bert finally back in bed, Kate stripped the dressings from his legs and grimaced as she saw what was underneath.

'Not improving?' The old man's eyes were on Kate's face.

'No, Bert, they're not,' she said honestly. She straightened and met his look. 'Bert, we're going to have to put you in hospital. Just for a few days,' she said quickly as she saw his face change. 'Once-a-day visits and dressing changes from the district nurse is not doing the trick.'

'What's the alternative?' Bert said sourly.

Once again Kate didn't flinch from his look. 'Bert, there's continued infection,' she said. 'If it gets any worse you risk amputation.'

'And if I don't agree to amputation I'll die,' the old man said. His voice was bitter. 'Well, you can just wrap

them up again, girl, and get the hell out of here. 'Cos if
they get me in some big city hospital I'll never get home
again, and you know that as well as I do. I'll die there
and I'd rather die here, in the valley, six months earlier
than in the city on me own.' He glared up at both
doctors.

Kate sighed and bent over the legs, carefully cleaning
and repacking the varicose ulcers. The legs were so thin
that the papery skin seemed as if it had nothing to
adhere to.

In her mind she was going through the possibilities.
They were bleak. Bert King was right. The nearest
hospital that would take him was a two-hour drive, too
far for any of his cronies to drop in for a visit. Bert's
brother lived over the hill from Bert, and was nearly as
frail. The two old men depended on each other for
everything.

'Why don't you and Sam live together?' Kate asked
mildly as she started bandaging. Bert gave a contemptuous snort.

''Cos we fight like cat and dog,' he said. 'Sam got
married early on. Damned fool idea if you ask me.
Didn't last more'n thirty years but it gave him all sorts
of nice ideas about scrubbing the bath out and squeezing the toothpaste from the end. I drive him nuts.'

Kate smiled. 'You might have to come to terms with
a different way of squeezing toothpaste,' she said
severely. 'It'd make a lot more sense.' She stood and
looked in concern down at the bed. 'After we get these
legs healed, that is.'

'I'm not going to any bloody hospital,' Bert snapped.

'Bert. . .'

'That's my last word.' The old man hauled himself
into a sitting position and glared. 'So you can get out,
Katy Harris. Thanks for your dressing. Now git!'

'If there were a hospital in Corrook could we per-
suade you to come in for a while?' Richard said

suddenly. He had been standing against the far wall listening, his face expressionless. The old man's eyes leapt to his.

'I heard rumours about that,' he said shortly. 'So you're serious.'

'Never more so.'

'Great words,' the old man jeered. 'I'll believe it when I see it.'

'How about being our first patient?'

Kate gasped and stared. 'Bert needs hospital now,' she said quickly.

'I know he does,' Richard said. He smiled down at the old man. 'Do you have health insurance?'

'I do,' Bert glared. 'For all the good it's ever done me. . .'

'Then there's no problem,' Richard smiled. 'I reckon we'll be ready for private patients within a week.' He stroked his chin thoughtfully. 'It could take longer for public patients. There's a darn sight more red tape.'

'You're kidding.' Kate and Bert were both staring at him as if he had lost his senses. Bert's words echoed Kate's thoughts.

'Nope.' Richard grinned. He delved into his pocket and produced a slip of paper. 'I've been working on this for some time. This is permission in principle from the health department to re-establish a ten-bed hospital in the valley. Their only stipulation is that we have two doctors available. I thought I'd set up practice and advertise, but it seems I don't have to.' He smiled down at Bert. 'Don't you think Dr Harris and I will make a good team?'

'But I'm leaving,' Kate said shortly. She felt as though the breath was being pushed from her body.

'Then we can't set up a hospital for Bert,' Richard told her, his expression bland. 'And I thought you were a caring doctor. . .'

'You can't walk out on the valley,' Bert told Kate.

His expression had lightened. Clearly the old man was enjoying the drama being played out before him. His old eyes flicked from Kate to Richard and back again, avid with curiosity.

Kate shook her head, totally out of her depth. She sought for control of the situation.

'Valley hospital or not, Bert needs hospital now,' she snapped. 'Dr Blair, those leg ulcers will be septic in a week. He can't wait until your pet project gets off the ground.' Her voice was angry. Richard Blair was starting to sound like a man air dreaming.

'You think I'm not serious, Dr Harris?' Richard Blair's voice was thoughtful.

'Of course I don't. A hospital within a week. . . The old Corrook hospital has been shut down and derelict for years. It's crazy.'

Richard looked down at Bert King. 'How about you, Bert? Do you believe me?'

The old man met his look. His eyes narrowed. Finally he nodded. 'Yes, I do, young fella,' he said slowly.

'Enough to go into hospital now in the city, with an absolute promise that we'll transfer you back to the valley as our hospital's first patient?'

The old man drew in his breath. So did Kate.

'You're asking a lot,' Bert said slowly.

'I know,' Richard agreed with a rueful smile. 'Absolute trust. Don't give it lightly.'

'I won't.'

Silence. The old man lay back on the pillows, his colour fading. He looked up to Kate.

'They really are getting worse?'

'They really are getting worse,' Kate said gently. 'I'm sorry, Bert. . .'

Bert fidgeted with the corner of his sheet. He moved his legs and winced with pain. Finally he looked over to Richard. 'A promise?' he demanded.

'A promise.'

The old man shoved out a hand towards Richard and Richard took it and gripped hard. 'Call me a bloody fool,' Bert said harshly, 'but I'll trust you.' He turned back to Kate. 'Arrange the bloody ambulance,' he told her. 'But if I die in that city hospital I'll come back and haunt the pair of you, you mark my words.'

Kate gave a reluctant smile. 'You're bad enough alive,' she teased him. 'Your ghost would be truly horrible.'

They left him chuckling. Kate shook her head in amazement as she walked down the front steps. To have Bert King agree to hospital and leave him smiling! Still. . .

She turned to Richard as they reached the car. 'You're mad,' she said in an undervoice.

Richard held up a warning finger and indicated the open bedroom window behind them. He said nothing, just ushered Kate into the passenger seat and started the car. Twenty yards from the house Kate finally found her tongue.

'You are, you know,' she said conversationally. 'Or cruel. I can't decide which.'

'Why?'

'Making promises you have no hope of keeping.'

'Why have I no hope of keeping them?'

'A hospital in a week,' Kate jeered. 'You have to be kidding.'

'I have the building,' Richard said seriously. 'It looks bad from the outside but it's structurally sound. I have the permission of the Health Department. I have orders for equipment. There's a team of builders starting on refurbishing even as we speak, and Alf says I only have to open my mouth locally to have half a dozen trained nurses vying for positions.'

Kate stared. Her jaw dropped and she fought for her voice. 'You're serious.'

'I'm serious. The only fly in the ointment was my lack

of another doctor. That's why I haven't started advertising for staff.'

'But this is crazy,' Kate gasped. 'You haven't even started work here.'

'And I don't intend to without a hospital,' Richard said firmly. 'Treating coughs and colds and sending anything more serious forty miles away to be treated by doctors I don't know is not my sort of medicine.'

'But it'll cost you a fortune!' Kate's mind was reeling.

'I've gone into the figures and I think I'll recoup. But I agree I'll run at a loss for a while.'

Kate sat back, stunned. The memories of some of Doug's crazy plans came into her mind. This man seemed just the same.

'It. . . It sounds ridiculous,' she said weakly.

'Ridiculous?' He flashed a smile across at her. 'I don't think so.'

'But spending all that money. . .'

'Oh, yes.' He nodded to himself and the smile faded. 'I forgot I'm speaking to the world's greatest miser. I gather I can't interest you in a partnership.'

Kate flushed and her hands gripped each other. 'I have no idea where you're getting your funds, but I certainly couldn't match them,' she said stiffly.

'The mattress not full enough?' he mocked her.

Kate bit her lip and said nothing.

The next patient was Mavis Souter. Mavis, like Bert, was in her eighties and lived alone. Unlike Bert's ramshackle cottage, though, Mavis's home was as neat as wax. Her tiny garden was a mass of annuals, no weed daring to inch its way above the surface. Her tiny home was newly painted, with 'Wee Hoose' carefully etched on the front gate, proclaiming the background of the woman within.

Richard and Kate were ushered into the spotless front parlour with ceremony. The old lady practically twittered.

'You should have told me you were bringing the new doctor,' she chided Kate gently, her breath coming in a whistling wheeze in her excitement. 'And I've only set for two. . .' She bustled off to the kitchen, ignoring the two doctors' involuntary protests.

The table was set with the best china. Cups, saucers, a magnificent teapot and matching crockery proclaimed high tea. There were scones, sandwiches and sponge cake.

'Now I see why you didn't want lunch,' Richard smiled.

'Miss Souter always does this,' Kate said softly. 'I call in whenever I can, but officially I visit once a month and she treats it as a state occasion. She'll be so pleased you've come.'

It was half an hour before they could leave, and only five minutes of that half-hour had been spent medically. Kate listened to the old lady's chest and checked her feet. 'Miss Souter has diabetes,' she told Richard. 'But she takes excellent care of herself.'

Mavis Souter nodded and beamed. 'I follow all the instructions,' she said proudly. 'Dr Harris has told me just what to do, and I'm so careful. . .'

Richard looked down to the leftover sponge cake on the table. 'What do you do with this, then?' he smiled.

'I throw it out,' Miss Souter said virtuously. And then she eyed him hopefully. 'Unless you'd like it, of course.' Her breath was drawn in.

'You couldn't throw it out,' Richard said, his voice shocked. 'What a waste. When there's needy bachelors like me pining for some home-cooking. . .'

Miss Souter's wrinkled face broke into a wreath of smiles. 'Oh, my dear. . .oh, of course. . .' She clucked away off to the kitchen to find some plastic wrap, and two minutes later Richard was stowing cake and scones into the boot of his car. Kate smiled as he lowered himself on to the driver's seat and restarted the engine.

'That's another visit to return the plates,' she warned him.

'I know it,' he grinned. 'It won't hurt me. Small payment for home-cooked sponge. . .'

Kate looked appraisingly at the man beside her. 'You realise you have a friend for life,' she told him. 'What's the bet when you go back there'll be plates of something else waiting?'

'I can cope,' Richard said expansively. He grinned. 'I might even enjoy it.' He turned his attention to the road. 'Is she as lonely as she seems?'

'More so. She has no one. Once a week, she takes a taxi into Corrook to do her shopping, and that's her only social outing. She has Meg, her cat, and nothing else.' Kate smiled reluctantly. 'She now has you.'

Richard nodded, as though he took the charge seriously. And Kate suddenly knew that he did. His request for sponge cake had nothing to do with his liking for the delicacy.

'How sick is she?' Richard asked.

'She has ischaemic heart disease, as well as emphysema,' Kate said. 'She's had three heart attacks over the years. One day I'll go up there and find her dead.' She shrugged. 'Like Bert, she shouldn't be alone, but the alternative is a nursing home forty miles away. And she really doesn't need a nursing home.'

Richard nodded. 'This place has an ageing population?' he queried.

'Very much so. Farming is less lucrative than it was thirty years ago, and more young people are choosing to leave. Lots of farms have combined, with one farmer owning one and leasing others, and the older farmers living their lives out in houses on leased land.'

Richard drummed his fingers on the steering-wheel. 'So what's the greatest need around here, as you see it?'

Kate was silent for a moment, thinking. Finally she

looked over to him. 'The hospital,' she said. 'That's obvious and I've wished that I could have done it. A hospital with nursing-home beds, so that old people like Bert can die in the valley. And also some sort of day-time activity centre for these people, with physiotherapy and occupational therapy and social interaction. Half my patients seem to be lonely. Living on an outlying farm by yourself can be pretty soul-destroying.'

Richard slowed as they neared the next patient's house. He frowned as he surveyed Kate.

'You don't have any money to put into this project, right?'

Kate took a deep breath. 'No,' she said.

Richard's frown increased. 'If we went into an asso-ciateship, would you be prepared to put a percentage of your income into the hospital?'

Kate thought of her mountain of bills, still outstand-ing. Her parents' house was still mortgaged. Kate's earnings were all that prevented her parents being forced to leave their home of forty years.

'No,' she said slowly. And then, as his face hardened, she said pleadingly, 'I can't. . .'

He shook his head, his expression still grim. 'Well, maybe it's just as well,' he said slowly. 'I'm not all that sure a professional partnership between us would work out.'

'I told you — I'm leaving,' Kate said shortly. 'I'm not asking for a share of your precious practice.'

'I'm not offering you one,' Richard retaliated. 'Not any more.' He was still drumming his fingers on the steering-wheel, deep in thought. 'How about a job?'

'A job?'

'A job,' Richard repeated. 'A no-strings-attached position, for a month only to start with. Cash in hand at the end of each week for you, which is what you seem to want, paid at medical association rates. Then at the end of the month, if we're no more impressed with each other than we are now, you can do what you want. Go back to working in opposition, or take a city job.'

'But I don't want to work for you,' Kate gasped.

'I know,' Richard said grimly. 'You want me to leave. Apologise profusely, withdraw from my contracts and get the hell out of here. Well, I would,' he said. 'I would if I thought there was a decent medical service in the town. But there's not, Dr Harris. You don't provide it and as far as I can see you have no intention of providing it. These people, the Miss Souters and the Bert Kings of this place, need a better deal, and I'm going to give it to them.'

'And go broke yourself in the attempt,' Kate said bitterly.

'I might,' Richard agreed. 'But at least I'll go broke trying to do something worthwhile, and as far as I can see that's a far better use of money than hoarding it. Now, do you want to work for me or not?'

'You can't possibly afford to pay me.'

'What I can afford is none of your business.'

'But it'll cost. . .'

'Do you want to work for me or not?'

'But I haven't a car,' Kate said weakly. 'I can't practise without a car.'

'For heaven's sake. . . You must be able to afford a car!'

'Well, I can't,' Kate told him, her face working. 'I told you—I'm broke. I. . . I got myself into financial trouble some time ago. . .'

A quick frown as Richard assimilated this. 'You're paying off debts?'

'Yes.' It was a whisper.

'You and the Corrook community. . .'

'That's not fair.'

He laughed without humour. 'Isn't it?'

'They didn't have a doctor at all until I came,' Kate

retorted, her anger rising. 'They were as desperate as . . .as I was.' Her voice trailed to silence.

'Desperate?'

Kate tried to meet his eyes and failed. They saw too much, those deep brown eyes. They held her, like a butterfly impaled on a pin. They were asking questions she had no wish to answer.

'I. . .' Her voice failed her and she tried again. 'I don't want to talk about my financial problems,' she pleaded.

'Do you want the job I'm offering, then?' he demanded.

'How can I keep practising with no car?' she burst out. 'I haven't a choice. I have to go back to the city.'

'I'll provide you with a car,' Richard said unexpectedly. 'Call it a perk of the job. We'll emblazon the side with "Corrook Valley Medical Service" if it'll make you happier.'

Kate stared at him. 'You're crazy,' she whispered. 'You're just throwing money around without a thought. Just like my. . .'

'Just like who?' Richard put his head to one side and looked at her.

Kate flushed, and turned away.

Richard sighed. 'Another question that's none of my business,' he said thoughtfully. 'I might have known.' He smiled suddenly. 'Never mind, Dr Harris. When you become my employee your personal secrets will be outed. You should see the dossiers I keep on my staff. Feet thick.'

Kate smiled despite herself. 'How many staff do you have?'

He appeared to consider. 'Let me see. For a start, do you accept this job or not?'

Kate hesitated. She met Richard's eyes. This man was crazy. He was working in a financial nightmare. She couldn't begin to understand how he could finance what he was proposing. And yet. . . And yet it was a dream she had been having since she had arrived here — to give the people of this valley medical service as it should be. How could she turn her back on such a project? And did she want to?

'I guess I do,' she said softly. She smiled. 'I'm probably as crazy as you, but I'll take on the job for a month.'

'Then my staff list has just grown dramatically,' Richard smiled. 'As of this moment, it stands at one.'

CHAPTER FOUR

THE next few days passed in a haze. Kate went to bed every night exhausted and woke every morning to the firm belief she had dreamed Richard's coming. He hit the valley like a whirlwind, leaving the town, and Kate in particular, stunned.

She saw him only briefly as he called in to her home to gather more information. She heard of him from everyone.

'You wouldn't believe what's happening down at the hospital,' Bella told her in a stunned whisper between patients. 'He has every able-bodied man in the district working on the site, I reckon.' She shook her head. 'I bet we'll have it done in time, too.'

'In time for what?' Kate asked, bemused.

'Didn't you know?' Bella said, horrified that her charge could have missed out on such vital information. 'Dr Blair has government permission to reopen the hospital but there's some question of a review of the procedures for granting licences. If we don't get it open by the end of the week we might miss out.'

Kate raised her eyebrows and said nothing. Back behind the closed door of her surgery she couldn't hide an appreciative smile. Richard Blair certainly knew how to get things done. This town wanted a hospital, and if they thought there was a chance they'd miss out Richard would have all the help he wanted. 'And I bet he's getting a lot of it free, too,' she said to herself, unable to suppress a twinge of jealousy. If she had only had the means to do this. . .

She looked out of the window at the gleaming little car in the car park, delivered the day after she had agreed to work with Richard. It had been delivered already emblazoned with the hospital logo. When she'd expressed amazement to the salesman he had shrugged his shoulders and grinned. 'Doc Blair said if we could do it in twenty-four hours we had a sale, otherwise he'd try somewhere else,' he told her. 'So here you are.'

Was there nothing the man wasn't capable of? Kate felt as if the breath was being pushed out of her. The valley health service was being turned on its ear.

And the valley loved it. One after another Kate's patients shook their heads in disbelief and told her how lucky the valley was.

'You must be so pleased,' they told her. 'To have him going into partnership with you. . .'

To her embarrassment Richard had clearly not spelled out the terms of Kate's employment to the community and had demanded that she not reveal them either. 'I want equal workloads,' he had told her brusquely when she protested. 'And if our patients aren't to differentiate between us, they have to see us as being equal. I'm paying you, Dr Harris, so we'll do this my way.'

So Kate just had to grit her teeth and accept congratulations on her good fortune.

She would have liked to see for herself what Richard was doing in the town, but for this week he was not seeing patients. Kate had to continue as sole general practitioner.

'I know you're exhausted,' Richard had told her. 'But if I take this week to get everything in order we can start on Monday as we mean to go on. And at least you have a car now. . .'

She did, and she had never worked so hard. It seemed as if everyone in the valley developed a symptom or two during the week, and three-quarters of them were, Kate guessed, attributable directly to a desire for gossip.

On Friday night she thankfully saw her last patient off the premises and then went through to her kitchen, sinking down exhausted at the kitchen table.

Bed, she thought longingly. It was all she wanted. What a week.

She should get herself something to eat but the effort of preparing a meal seemed too much trouble. It was often the way in the evening. She was too thin, she knew, but cooking seemed just too hard.

With Doug, life had been one long round of social meals. Now, for instance. . .on Friday nights. . . If there wasn't some social gathering planned, Doug would organise one, usually at the city's most expensive restaurant. Staying at home on a Friday night was unthinkable.

The sound of a car's wheels on the gravel outside made Kate lift her head. She was almost asleep where she sat. She glanced out of the window to see Richard Blair striding towards the house.

It was raining, a soft drizzle that was almost dew, but steady enough to wet him on his way into the house. As Kate opened the back door to admit him he gave himself a shake. In his moleskins and the big, hand-knitted sweater he obviously lived in, he reminded Kate of nothing as much as a large, dependable bear.

Dependable? The word flew into her mind and she could not shake it off. Why? Was it just the fact that he was so large? Or was it her loneliness, doing strange things to her emotions?

'Sorry for turning up at this hour.' Richard was smiling his apology down to her. 'I've been in the city collecting more supplies, and it took longer than I thought to unload the truck.'

'Truck?' Kate looked outside to where Richard's Mercedes was parked.

'I followed the delivery truck back,' Richard said. 'It

was jam-packed. Everything from washing machines to bedpans.'

Kate stared up at him. 'You really are serious about getting the hospital open by Monday.'

'I sure am,' Richard told her. 'The painters finished yesterday and the floor coverings went in this morning. I had every available pair of hands in Corrook cleaning there this afternoon. The place is gleaming.' He smiled. 'The valley is buzzing with enthusiasm. All I'm doing is harnessing it. The health inspector's visit is scheduled for nine a.m. on Monday and Bert King arrives back from the city by ambulance on Monday afternoon. I dropped in to see him while I was in the city and he's looking forward to it.'

Kate stared. 'But the nursing staff. . .' she said weakly.

'Starting on Monday,' Richard said evenly. 'Officially, that is. Unofficially they've been working most of the week. As Alf said, all I had to do was open my mouth and suggest there were jobs available. It's a skeleton staff at first. I've only been able to locate six registered nurses who want work, and I'm going to need more than that when the hospital finds its feet, but one, Alma Wishart, is a triple-certificated sister, and is delighted to be matron, and Janet Harley is happy with night supervision.'

Kate nodded, still stunned. She knew both Alma and Janet. Both women had been desperate to get back to nursing for years, but as they were married to local farmers it had never been an option.

'I don't know how you've managed it,' she whispered. She still felt as if she was asleep and dreaming.

'By sheer hard work,' Richard grinned. He crossed the kitchen and opened the refrigerator before Kate could protest. 'Or, to be honest, by sheer hard supervision. Either way, I need a drink.'

'And by waving wads of money,' Kate said waspishly.

Richard's grin deepened. 'There is that,' he conceded. 'It must really hurt to see me splashing it around.' He sighed. 'What I really want here, Dr Harris, is a beer. All I'm seeing is half a limp lettuce, a loaf of bread and some cheese. Something tells me that you're not the sort of woman to keep a second fridge. Is this it?'

'It?'

'All your house runs to in the way of provisions?'

'There's water in the tap,' Kate said defensively.

'Well, I'm not drinking water,' Richard said decisively. 'Not after the week I've had.' He looked over to her and frowned. 'And you've had a hell of a week too. Those shadows under your eyes have deepened since Monday.'

'I'm fine.'

'Have you had dinner?'

'I'll have some when you leave,' Kate said.

'What?'

'I. . . I beg your pardon?'

'What are you going to eat?' he demanded bluntly. 'Cheese sandwiches with limp lettuce? Is that the way you celebrate Friday nights?'

Kate stiffened. 'I don't celebrate Friday nights,' she said coldly.

He nodded, his eyes appraising the too thin girl with the strained eyes and shadows. She looked haunted, he thought, his brows coming together in a frown. As if the shadows were chasing her. . .

'Well, you'll celebrate this one,' he said with decision. He walked to the door and held it open. 'Get your coat.'

'M-my coat?'

'You're not deaf, Dr Harris,' he said. 'Your coat. Or your mink stole if you run to it.' His tone was laced with sarcasm and Kate flushed.

'I can't go out,' she said. 'I'm on call.'

'Tonight I'm on call,' Richard said. He lifted a small black case from his pocket and snapped it open. 'A mobile telephone. I can link it to your phone so whenever anyone rings it buzzes in my pocket.' He smiled. 'So there you are, Dr Harris. All your responsibilities placed in my pocket. What girl could ask for more?'

'But I don't want to go out.' It was practically a wail. Kate was feeling the ground being eroded from under her feet. She was out of control, and she didn't like it. She had the same breathless, horrified feeling she had experienced when Doug had come home with yet another exciting venture to lay before her. And this man. . . She glanced up at his eyes, a hint of laughter in their depths and a challenge. Yes, certainly a challenge. He was so different from Doug, and yet the same. To do what he was doing was mad. . .

'I don't want to go,' she repeated weakly.

'I'm not asking what you want,' Richard Blair said firmly. 'You're employed by me, and as far as I can see you're starving yourself into oblivion. If you insist on being a bloody fool, then you'll be treated like one. There's things we need to talk about. I'm hungry and I'm damned if I'll eat limp lettuce. Get your coat and get into my car or I'll pick you up and carry you. Now, Dr Harris. Before I lose my temper.'

'I don't have to. . .' Kate looked up and met his eyes, and what she saw there made her hesitate. This man was making no idle threat. He meant what he said. His eyes gave her that promise.

Her alternative was to tell him to get out and stay out, and that meant the end of her life in this valley. And it also meant the end of her time with Richard Blair.

Did she want that? Yes, her head was screaming at her. Yes, yes. But then those eyes caught her and she was held, and something twisted deep within, some-

thing that she thought had died the night she knew
Doug had left her for another woman. And she wanted
it to be dead, she thought savagely. She would never
again expose herself to that pain — to that betrayal.

'Well?' Richard asked. He was still holding the door
open.

'I'll come,' Kate said coldly. 'But I'll follow you in
my car.'

'Whose car?'

'The car I'm using,' Kate snapped. 'There's no need
to rub it in, Dr Blair. I'm dependent on you and you
know it. You say hop and I have to hop. But I don't
have to like it. Now let's get this damned dinner over
with.' She grabbed her coat from the back of a chair
and stalked out of the room.

Two minutes later Kate was following the tail-lights
of the big silver Mercedes down the rough track towards
the town. She assumed they were heading down to the
only dinner commercially available in Corrook — the
counter tea from the Corrook pub. A mile down,
however, the big Mercedes slowed and indicated a
right-hand turn. To Kate's horror she realised Richard
Blair was going home.

She didn't turn with him. She pulled her little car
over to the side of the road and stopped, then sat
staring out into the night. Moments later Richard
realised she was not following. The Mercedes backed
down the track leading to his house, Richard climbed
out of the car and came across to open her car door.

'Car trouble, Dr Harris?'

'I thought we were going to the pub,' Kate said
quietly.

'Assumptions are dangerous things,' he said pleasantly. 'They can get you in all sorts of trouble. But in
this case there's no problem. Simply a reassessment of
the situation, a deft pull of the wheel to the right and

the thing's done. Surely a woman with a degree in medicine can handle that.'

Kate flushed. 'There's no need to patronise me,' she said angrily.

'And there's no need to get your knickers in a knot because things don't turn out as you planned,' Richard said evenly.

'Well, why aren't we going to the pub?' Kate's voice contained a hint of desperation.

'Because if it's like any country pub I've ever been to on a Friday night it will be packed with locals celebrating just that — Friday night,' he told her. 'And I want to talk business. It's not the place to do it. My refrigerator is a lot healthier than yours, and I can even cook.' He grimaced. 'Dr Harris, it's starting to rain. Would you mind if we continued this conversation indoors?' And he left her, striding swiftly back to his car.

Kate hesitated for a moment and then reluctantly switched on her ignition. It seemed there was nothing to do but follow.

Richard nosed his car into the garage and then emerged to wait for her. He stood patiently, a tall, dark shadow, as she parked her car under the bank of acacias near the house. The big red gum she carefully avoided. The red gums were lovely but they had a nasty habit of shedding limbs unexpectedly. If Richard's new little car was squashed he'd simply go out and buy another, though, she thought maliciously. The man was spending money as if he had a licence to manufacture it.

'Is this car insured?' she asked as she emerged from the car. Richard didn't move from where he stood, waiting for her to approach.

'Of course it is.' Laughter was back in his voice. It was never absent for long, Kate thought wonderingly. Life was a pleasure for Richard Blair. 'Do you think I'd let a woman who demonstrated her car care by blowing up her last one get within an ace of mine without insurance?' He grinned as she reached him. 'I might be a spendthrift, Dr Harris, but I'm not a fool.'

Kate caught her breath. 'I didn't say you were a spendthrift,' she said tightly.

'You didn't have to.' Richard took her arm and guided her up the rough steps leading to the house. 'I can read it in your eyes.' The laughter deepened in his voice. 'I told you I took elementary psychology. Reading eyes is what I'm good at.' His grip tightened as she stumbled. 'Sorry about the path. I need some exterior lighting.' He looked ruefully up at the house they were approaching. 'In fact I need a few things, but they'll have to wait. I seem to have exhausted Corrook's labour supply as it is.' They reached the top step as he spoke, crossed the wide veranda and Richard flung open the front door.

The few things Richard needed weren't obvious to Kate. She walked in to the big living-room and stopped in amazement as Richard flicked on the light switch.

The man had only been living in the place a little over a week and already it seemed like a home. Kate had been in the house previously. When she had first arrived in the valley old Mrs Stevenson had still been living in the house. Two weeks after the old lady died Kate had called to pick up a nebuliser she had left with her. The relatives had moved in and stripped the place bare. Now. . . Kate stared around in amazement at the comfortable, homey furniture, the generous Persian rugs thrown over the bare boards, the paintings on the walls, bookcases crammed with books. . . There was even a fire burning in the hearth.

'I thought you'd been in Melbourne all day,' she said accusingly.

Richard raised his eyebrows. 'Would I lie to you?' he said in a wounded tone. 'My cleaning lady's been in.'

'Your cleaning lady. . .'

'Don't sound so surprised. Doesn't everyone have a

cleaning lady?' he asked innocently. He had crossed through to the kitchen. Through the open door Kate saw him open the refrigerator door and pull out a bottle of wine, then stand, considering. Finally he returned the wine to the fridge and replaced it with champagne.

'No, they do not,' she said waspishly. 'And they don't have mansions to live in when they've only been in the valley for a week.'

'Oh, come now.' The champagne cork emerged with a healthy pop. Richard came through to the living-room with champagne and two glasses. 'A three-bed-room weatherboard house with one bathroom is hardly a mansion. I don't even have a bidet. I'd like to know how a house can call itself a mansion without a bidet.'

Kate choked. She looked up at Richard and for the first time for months her sense of humour reasserted itself. Her laughing eyes met his, and his deep brown eyes warmed. He poured a glass of champagne and handed it to her.

'I shouldn't drink.' Kate took the glass and eyed it doubtfully.

'I told you,' Richard said firmly. 'Your responsibili-ties are in my pocket.' He patted the mobile phone. 'Tonight I'm on call. After two glasses of champagne I revert to mineral water.'

Kate sighed. Deep within, the heavy load of responsi-bility she had been carrying since Doug had walked out shifted, and when it resettled it was lighter. She took a sip of champagne, but she didn't need it. She was faintly giddy without it.

'Now,' Richard said firmly. 'Dinner. Come into the kitchen and talk to me while I cook.'

'Can you really cook?' Kate demanded.

'Can a fish swim?' Richard demanded. 'Of course.' Then, seeing the look on her face, he relented. 'I can cook steak, sausages, mashed potatoes or chips. I also make excellent coffee and I am considered a true cordon bleu chef when it comes to TV dinners. Therein lies my total repertoire.'

They had steak. Richard cooked it to perfection, while Kate perched on the edge of the big, polished table and watched him. He refused all offers of help with his customary light banter.

'To imply I need help is the worst form of insult. Keep your help for when it's needed, woman.'

So Kate subsided into her champagne, sipped, watched and listened.

The banter slipped as Richard started talking of his plans. The laughter faded from his voice and Kate's incomprehension deepened.

She was accustomed to listening to dreams. Doug's head had been filled with dreams for their entire marriage. The dream she was listening to now, though, was different. For the first time she saw that Richard Blair's involvement was not a whim. It was the embodiment of something he had dreamed of for years, and the dream was backed by hard practicalities.

She listened as he described the structure he envisaged for the hospital — the shifts and rosters for nursing and cleaning staff. He had regular theatre times planned and emergency procedures tentatively worked out. He had already sounded out the local support services and had spent time in Melbourne investigating the possibility of expanding the ambulance service.

'Because if we get a solid service here, one ambulance driver on twenty-four-hour call will be worked into the ground,' he said seriously. 'I've already put a notice in the local paper asking for volunteer emergency drivers.'

'You envisage the demand starting this early,' Kate said wonderingly.

'It will.' Richard flipped the steak and turned to the bench to slice some onions. 'I need to know what you're happy to handle. Obs?'

'I have my obstetric diploma,' Kate said. 'But we won't be given birth-unit status.'

'We might because of our isolation,' Richard said. 'And I'm perfectly capable of doing a Caesar.'

Kate shook her head. 'We need three doctors. If we haven't a paediatrician on stand-by it's not fair to agree to do them.'

'But we can do them in an emergency,' Richard said firmly. 'We don't have to send a woman for a two-hour ambulance drive knowing there'll be a dead baby at the end of it.'

'No.' Kate thought back to an incident three months ago. One of the local farmer's wives had called her in the small hours of the morning. Kate had arrived at the outlying farm to realise the woman was in labour, and in fact had been labouring for days. Her face must have changed because Richard laid down his knife.

'Want to tell me about it?' he asked.

Kate shook her head. 'I was just wishing you'd been here three months ago,' she said simply. 'I lost a baby.'

'But the mids here go to the city.'

'They're supposed to,' Kate told him. 'But they can't be forced, and for many women it's just not an option. They have nowhere in the city to stay for the weeks before the baby's due and many have families dependent on them. So they stay and run the risks.'

Richard nodded. 'And sometimes it doesn't pay off.'

'No.'

Richard turned back to his steak, throwing in the onions and searing them swiftly. Then he deftly slid steak and onions on to the plates, loaded the plates with vegetables and placed them on the table.

'Dinner is served,' he said solemnly. 'Beats a cheese sandwich any day.'

Kate had to agree it did. The steak melted in her mouth and it gave her a shock to realise just how long it was since she had eaten one. She had been living on cheese sandwiches, mince and cheap vegetables for years. As for wine. . . She opened her eyes wide as Richard took the cork from a bottle of claret.

'Not just for me,' she protested.

Richard smiled. 'Just for you,' he said firmly. 'I've succeeded in making you smile. I intend to keep you that way.'

'I don't need wine to make me smile,' Kate told him.

'Then what do you need?' His eyes were watchful, appraising.

Kate bent her eyes to her steak. She was warm, seemingly for the first time in weeks, and the food and wine was spreading a warm glow within her. Her house was furnished with the bare essentials, with anything of any worth long since sold. This place. . . It was warm, secure and comforting.

Like Richard, she thought suddenly, and then flung the thought away. Richard Blair wasn't comforting. He was just as big a fool as Doug, even if his dreaming was more practical. It was just as crazy a dream. To spend money the way he had. . .

'It's slipped,' Richard said slowly.

'Pardon?'

'Your smile's slipped. It was there one minute and now it's gone. What were you thinking of to make your smile slip?'

Kate shrugged. 'I was thinking how much you've been spending,' she said quietly. 'And I was wondering how long you could keep it up.'

Richard's eyes narrowed. 'Why so concerned?' he asked. 'Surely it's nothing to do with you if I go broke?'

'It is my business,' Kate said with some asperity. 'The valley people are due for a dreadful disappointment when the crash comes.'

'And you think the crash is inevitable.'

'No one can spend as much as you and not get their fingers burnt.'

'Can't they?' Richard was fingering his glass, idly watching the girl across the table. His finger ran around the rim of the crystal, and the glass hummed. In the next room the fire crackled and spat. As if coming to a decision, Richard stood up and held out a hand. 'Coffee by the fire,' he said.

'I must be getting home. . .'

'After coffee.' He took her hand firmly in his and led her through to the fire.

Kate sat on the big leather settee, watching the pile of blazing logs as Richard prepared the coffee in the kitchen. She looked down at her hand, still warm from Richard's clasp, and a matching warm flush crept into her face. She shouldn't be here.

Her hand rested on her serviceable skirt, and her plain black shoes looked out of place on the plush Persian rug. Richard Blair should be entertaining a woman of style here, she thought bitterly. Such a setting was wasted on her. She looked up as he entered the room and tried to match his smile. His faded. Putting the cup of fragrant brewed coffee into her hands, he sank to sit beside her. Once again Kate was overwhelmed by his size. He made her feel small, and no man had ever done that to her. He made her feel. . .

Richard Blair made her feel as if she ought to stand and flee — get the hell out of there while there was still time. Something was going on within her that she didn't understand at all — didn't want to understand. Her heart was doing headstands, just because this big, fair-haired man with the kind smile and the all-knowing eyes was sitting beside her.

It's his bedside manner, she told herself breathlessly. I'll bet all the old ladies just love him.

'Kate. . .'

Kate caught herself as he spoke. She looked up and met his eyes and then wished she hadn't. She stared firmly down at her feet.

'Kate, why on earth are you so miserable?'

'I'm not miserable.'

'Well, why can't I make you laugh?'

'You can. You did.'

'Once. And I had to work damned hard to get that.
And then you reverted straight back to my spendthrift
habits.'

'Can I help it if I disapprove?'

'Is it just me you disapprove of, Dr Harris, or is it
men in general?'

Kate caught her breath and her coffee slopped over
the side of her mug. She wiped the drops angrily from
her skirt. 'Don't be ridiculous,' she said harshly.

'Am I being ridiculous?' He sat back and eyed her
speculatively. 'What's a lovely woman like you doing
hiding in the back-blocks under a mountain of debt?
Wounded in love, eh, Kate?'

'Dr Harris, to you,' Kate told him. She rose and the
coffee slopped again. 'I have to go home.'

He rose with her. Before she could step away,
though, he had taken the coffee-mug from her lifeless
fingers and placed it on the mantel. Then he turned and
cupped her face in his hands.

'What's hurting you, Kate? What's making you like a
wounded animal, snarling at all the world? I'm not out
to hurt you, you know.'

'You'll hurt this valley.'

'How will I hurt this valley?'

'With your big spending and your grandiose schemes
and your cruel promises. . .' Kate broke off as tears
came into her eyes. 'You can't possibly afford to do
what you're doing for long. You'll just get the valley
believing and go bust, or do a bunk with a mountain of
debt.' She shook her head. 'It's crazy.'

'Isn't it just possible that you're wrong?'

Kate shrugged. 'I know what it costs to run a private

hospital. Do you think I haven't dreamed of reopening it myself one day? I know the figures. . .'

Richard's look softened. His hands caught hers and his eyes held her. 'It's not crazy,' he said softly. 'Kate, believe me, I'm not doing this without knowing exactly what I'm letting myself in for. I've done my homework. This has a good chance of succeeding.'

Kate tugged at her hands. 'A good chance,' she mocked. 'So you admit there's a chance you'll fail.'

His hands tightened. 'Yes,' he said gravely. 'There is. If my estimates are wrong. If the locals don't use the hospital. If there's flood, fire or pestilence. . .' He stopped and smiled wryly. 'Well, maybe pestilence would be OK, as long as you and I don't succumb. Pestilence involving nice long hospital stays could suit us very nicely. . .'

Kate tugged her hands again. 'I'm serious,' she managed to say. 'Why can't you be?'

Her hands were still held and there was silence. Richard said nothing. Finally Kate looked up to meet his eyes and found him waiting. He had wanted her to look at him.

'It's a risk worth taking,' he said. 'It's a dream that I'm putting every part of me into. And I'd like you to share it with me, Kate. If not financially, at least with your heart.'

'M-my heart?'

'With yourself. If we both try. . .' He shook his head. 'I can't do it alone, Kate, and I have a feeling that if I don't have your faith it's not going to work. For the valley to use us, they have to believe in what we're doing. And if one of us thinks it's a venture doomed to failure, we'll never get off the ground.'

'So that's why you brought me here. To fill me with your crazy vision.'

'That's right.' His mouth twisted as he looked down at her. 'For no other reason. . .' He stood, staring down at the dark shadows around her eyes. Her hands still lay in his. And then, slowly, as though driven by an irresistible force, he bent his lips to kiss her.

And for one crazy, crazy moment, Kate responded. It must have been fatigue, she told herself later, desperately seeking justification. Fatigue and the loneliness and desperation of the past few months. . . But the feel of his lips on hers, his strong hands holding hers, and the warmth and laughter in his deep brown eyes. His warmth. . . It caught at the trails of loneliness and held her, making her want above all else to raise her hands, to hold the fair head to hers and to deepen the kiss. To deepen the dreaming. . . Her mouth tasted his maleness and her body wanted him. . .

And then the dreaming snapped. A moment's madness—that was all it was. And she was pushing him away, her green eyes flashing fire.

'How dare you? What do you think you're doing?' She stepped back and glared, her breath coming in ragged gasps.

His eyes held laughter, but now something else—a trace of uncertainty?

'I would have thought it was obvious what I was doing.' He put a finger up to trace the outline of her cheek. 'I'm kissing a beautiful woman.'

Kate laughed scornfully. 'A beautiful woman. . . You have to be joking.' She glanced down at her serviceable skirt and dowdy cardigan. 'I don't know what you want, Dr Blair, but you're flattering the wrong woman.' She grabbed her coat from the back of the chair. 'I'm leaving.'

His hand moved to grasp her arm. Still there was the look of uncertainty in his eyes.

'If you don't think you're beautiful you haven't looked in the mirror lately,' he said softly. 'Kate. . .'

'Leave me alone!' She wrenched her arm back, her

eyes failing to meet his. She couldn't look at his eyes. She couldn't look and not want. . . Not want. . .

She was going mad.

She turned to leave, and as she did the shrill tones of the mobile phone broke the stillness.

Kate took two steps towards the door and then stopped. The last years had made her a servant of the phone. Her life was controlled by it. It could mean an emergency, and she was all the medical service the valley had.

Not any more she wasn't, she reminded herself harshly. This man was assuming control.

But she couldn't leave. She had to know. She stood, her coat slung over her shoulder, her breath still coming too fast, as Richard Blair spoke into the phone.

'Corrook Medical Service.' He smiled across at Kate as he said the words. From here on in, it seemed, they were in business.

Silence. The smile faded from Richard's eyes and his brows snapped together.

'Get as much pressure on it as possible. Wrap it up tight, as tight as you can. Fast.' He turned to Kate. 'Do you know the way to Bill Mannaway's farm?'

Kate nodded mutely and Richard turned back to the phone.

'Keep that pressure up and keep her warm. Nothing else. We'll be there as soon as we can.' He was moving towards the door as he flicked the phone closed, and Kate was practically pushed outside.

'Wh-what. . .?'

'Emergency,' Richard snapped. 'Let's go.'

CHAPTER FIVE

'WHAT . . . what is it?' Kate said breathlessly. Five seconds later they were off the veranda. Richard had caught her hand and was running towards the car, supporting her on the rough ground but still running.

'Your gear's in your boot?' he demanded. Kate nodded and Richard flung out a hand for the keys.

'My car's faster.' He threw open Kate's luggage compartment, grabbed her bulky case and tossed it into the back seat of his Mercedes. Kate wordlessly climbed into the passenger seat. Whatever was happening she would know soon enough, and Richard's pressure on her hand had told her he needed her.

'Tell me where to go,' Richard demanded, not looking at her. The big car sprang to life, lurched back out of the garage, swung around and headed for the road gate.

'Into town and turn left. The Mannaways' farm is about two miles out on the main road.'

He nodded and flung the moblie phone across to her. 'Ring the ambulance,' he said. 'Tell them to meet us up there, and tell them to stop at the hospital on the way for as much plasma as we have.'

'Plasma. . .'

'It's already here, thank God,' Richard said devoutly. 'I ordered supplies.'

'The ambulance always carries some,' Kate said quietly.

'Not enough for this,' Richard said grimly.

Kate looked a question but Richard's attention was wholly on the road. Kate turned to the phone.

Richard didn't speak again as he negotiated the bends

in the rough road. After the phone call to the ambulance Kate sat silently as well. The car was cutting through the night like a silver bullet. As Richard neared the main road he put his hand on the horn and left it there, hard. It would be heard miles away, Kate thought, warning any vehicle that they were in a hurry.

Finally they were on the stretch of smooth bitumen leading away from the town. Richard's foot hit the floor and stayed there, and the moonlit farmland passed in a blur. Kate looked across at his grim, set face. She had never driven this fast in her life, but this man was in control. He wasn't afraid of speed. He was taking no foolish risks, but he wanted to get there fast.

'Can you tell me?' she said quietly.

Richard's eyes didn't leave the road. 'Sophie Mannaway. Do you know her?'

Kate nodded. 'A child. Ten or so. A pretty little thing with long red hair. . .'

'Not any more,' Richard said grimly. 'She caught her hair in the drive belt of the milking machine. Her father says she's been scalped.'

Kate's breath caught in her throat. 'Scalped. . .'

'It's been ripped off,' Richard said, and his voice wasn't quite even. 'I've never. . .' His voice died away and the car flew through the night.

'It mightn't be as bad as it sounds,' Kate said quietly. 'If the hair's been ripped from the scalp. . .'

'That's not what Bill Mannaway said happened. The scalp itself has been torn.'

They didn't speak again. There was nothing to be said. There was nothing to do except get to the farm as soon as they could.

The inevitable dogs met them at the farm gate but the door was closed and no one appeared as the car drew up. As they emerged from the car and ran towards the house, the back door opened and a child's frightened face appeared. Kate recognised Luke, Sophie's younger brother.

'Where's Sophie, Luke?' she asked gently. The little boy's face was as white as a sheet.

'She's. . . She's in the kitchen. Dad says. . . Dad says come through. . .'

They didn't need telling twice. Richard was already in. Kate took the scared little boy's hand in hers and followed.

The kitchen looked like a scene from a dreadful war movie. There was blood everywhere they looked. Mrs Mannaway sat in a kitchen chair, cradling the dreadfully injured little girl to her. She was sobbing, her body heaving in her terror. Beside her, Bill Mannaway was wrapping more towels tightly round the child's head, his face reflecting blank hopelessness.

'She's close to unconsciousness,' he said dully. 'And she's hardly breathing.'

Richard was already bending over the child, his hand on her pulse.

'Drip,' he snapped to Kate. 'Fast.'

He grabbed a couple of towels from the table and spread them out on its surface. Then he took the limp figure from the woman's shuddering grasp.

'We'll do what we can,' he told her. 'There's nothing more you can do.' He gestured to the little boy behind them. 'Mrs Mannaway, your little boy needs you.' His eyes held hers and she caught her breath on a sob of terror.

'Sophie'll die.'

'Go and shower and change and get yourself back to normal,' he told her. 'Your son stands a good chance of going into shock if he sees your terror. And when Sophie wakes, she has to see the mum she knows and loves.' His eyes held hers. 'We'll look after her,' he assured her.

The woman stared at him wildly. Then the little boy

grabbed her blood-soaked skirt and pulled. 'Mummy. . .' he said desperately.

With a huge effort the woman fought for and found control.

'OK, Luke,' she smiled weakly. 'The doctors will look after Sophie. Mummy can get herself clean again.' She took the little boy and left the room.

Kate had the saline drip out of her case before the woman had left the room. Richard was already swabbing a forearm. He held out a hand for the needle and inserted it without acknowledging its receipt.

'What happened?' he demanded as he worked. Behind him, the farmer was standing uncertainly.

'I. . . I was just finishing milking,' the farmer said. 'The cows had been skittish — I'm breaking in a new pup and he'd made 'em nervous — and Marg sent Sophie over to see what was keeping me.' He swallowed convulsively. 'She knows. . .she knows to keep away from the belts. Usually she has her hair in plaits but she'd just had her bath. It must have caught as she went past. Next thing I heard was screams. . .'

Richard nodded. He was starting very gently to remove the blood-soaked towels.

'Can you turn the outside light on for the ambulance?' he asked. 'And you could wait outside too, if you like. Dr Harris and I can cope.'

'But. . .she'll be OK?'

'I don't know,' Richard said softly. 'But we'll do our damnedest.'

The farmer closed his eyes. His shoulders slumped and he left the room.

There was silence. Kate had the saline drip full on, trying desperately to raise the child's blood-pressure. She found bowls in the cupboard near the stove, and filled them with steaming water from the huge black kettle. When she came back to the table Richard scrubbed swiftly and removed the last of the towels.

Kate drew in her breath, and then took hold of herself. Once horror took hold, objectivity went out the window, she told herself grimly.

At least she wasn't alone. How she would have coped. . . Richard's fingers were skilled and sure as they carefully examined the oozing wound.

Under their hands the child stirred and whimpered. Kate's face lightened. She moved swiftly to administer pain-killers, carefully working around Richard's probing fingers. That the little girl was conscious was a good sign. The only good sign. . .

The light above their heads was a brilliant, naked globe, but Kate augmented it with a strong torch from her case. The blood was still oozing down the child's forehead. Richard grimaced up at Kate and Kate had artery forceps ready for him. Swiftly he raised the flap of torn flesh. Kate moved in with swabs while he tied off the spurting arteries. As the bleeding subsided he replaced the torn flesh and applied a compression bandage to the whole area.

They were working well, almost soundlessly, together. It wasn't the theatre Kate would have chosen, but it was all they had. She monitored the child's feeble breath, adjusted the drip and listened for the sound of the ambulance. She wanted plasma.

Finally she heard the wail of the ambulance siren. Joe had taken his time, she thought, and then bit back the criticism. Joe was the only driver the valley had, and he couldn't be behind the wheel ready to go twenty-four hours a day seven days a week. He had probably been down at the local when the call came through, enjoying a convivial Friday night.

He came in flustered, ushered through by a frightened Mrs Mannaway. The woman cast a scared glance down at her daughter and whisked herself out again. Clearly she was finding it difficult to stay in control.

Joe was carrying what Kate most desperately wanted.

With relief she took the plasma from Joe's hand and raised it above the little girl. Now, if Richard could only stop the bleeding. . .

'I can't do any more here,' Richard said. 'The rest will have to be done under a general anaesthetic.'

Joe looked from one doctor to the other. 'We'll take her to Melbourne, then?'

Richard shook his head. 'There's still too much bleeding,' he said firmly. 'I've tied off the main arteries but there's scores of minor ones which won't close until we get that flap stitched down. I'd prefer a plastic surgeon to do the stitching, but Sophie wouldn't make the trip.' He looked down to the limp little girl on the table.

'Sophie, can you hear me?'

'Mmm.' It was a frightened, hurt little whimper.

'Sophie,' he said softly, 'you've cut your head — a really big cut. We need to pull the edges together so you won't have a nasty scar. Mr Vincent's going to take you for a ride in his ambulance.' Richard's hand was on the bloodstained little face, stroking the white cheek. 'You know we have a new hospital. You're going to be its first patient.'

Sophie didn't answer. Her eyes closed. Whether she had heard they couldn't tell, but at least she seemed calm.

And how much of that calmness could be attributed to shock and blood-loss? Kate wondered grimly. She took Sophie's blood-pressure again and winced. 'I didn't think the hospital was ready,' she said softly.

'It's not.' Richard's voice was just as quiet. 'But it's Sophie's only chance. Joe and I will take her down. You ring round the nurses. I want three in there tonight. Tell them their future employment's on the line. Then follow us down in my car.' He tossed her his car keys, and motioned to Joe. 'Bring in the stretcher.'

Fifteen minutes later Kate drew up in front of the

hospital, switched off the ignition of the unfamiliar car and stared in amazement. A week ago this building had been dilapidated and deserted. Now. . .

Now it was a thriving, living hospital, its light streaming across the still neglected grounds, an ambulance drawn up in front of a brightly lit casualty sign and two other cars in the car park. As Kate emerged from the Mercedes another car swung in and drew to a halt. Kate recognised Alma Wishart, Richard's newly employed matron. Kate stared. She had phoned this lady less than ten minutes ago. Alma hurried towards her, doing up the buttons on her starched white uniform as she came.

'I don't believe it. . .' Kate shook her head and Alma beamed.

'You did say it was an emergency,' she said primly. She took Kate's hand. 'Oh, Dr Harris, it's just so good to be needed again.'

That seemed to be the consensus of the entire nursing staff. Kate had rung three nurses, but by the time they had Sophie prepped and ready for Theatre the entire hospital nursing staff of five were present. News of a drama like this travelled fast in the valley.

It meant they had a full theatre contingent, with staff left over to prepare the ward and do final cleaning.

'It's just as well we had the theatre sterile before I left yesterday,' Alma said as they wheeled Sophie in. She looked around in satisfaction. 'I said to myself it was silly to have a theatre only half finished. It was as if I knew. . .'

Kate was having trouble believing her eyes. When Alma wheeled in the anaesthetic trolley she shook her head in disbelief. Here was everything she needed. Everything. . .

It was just as well. Sophie's blood-pressure was continuing to drop.

Kate adjusted the plasma flow and moved to help Richard before giving the final anaesthetic. Sophie lay passive and unmoving beneath their hands. Her very stillness frightened Kate.

She opened her eyes as Kate produced a pair of scissors.

'What. . .what are you going to do?' she whispered.

'I'm giving you a haircut,' Kate said reassuringly. She snipped the long, tangled locks from the torn head.

'I don't. . . I don't think I want a haircut. . .' Sophie started to weep soundlessly. At a signal from Richard, Kate moved back to administer the anaesthetic. If Sophie were to become upset it would be better to finish it while she was asleep.

'Not even if I give it to you?' Richard said teasingly. He picked up the scissors and kept on where Kate had left off. 'Do you know I've just come from London? I've even seen Buckingham Palace.' He smiled down at Sophie's tear-stained face. 'And short hair is all the go in London. All the prettiest models have lovely smart haircuts, all cut short. Just as yours is going to be. Even Princess Di has short hair.'

'Princess Di. . .'

'Surely you've heard of Princess Di?' Teasing laughter was back in Richard's voice. 'Don't you learn anything in Australian schools?'

'I know who Princess Di is!' The weak voice sounded indignant and Richard grinned.

'Pretty or not pretty?' he demanded.

Sophie considered. 'Pretty,' she finally decided. Kate's anaesthetic was starting to take effect and her voice came from a long way away.

'Well, there you are, then, miss. You'll be the wearer of the height of London fashion. Courtesy of Dr Blair's fantastic haircutting service. . .' Richard's voice faded off as Sophie slept.

'OK.' Richard's voice changed swiftly. 'Let's move. She's in no condition to take any more anaesthetic than is absolutely essential.'

They moved. For a team who had never worked together—for nurses who hadn't worked for years—they welded together in amazing unity. Somehow the sterilised instruments were placed in Richard's or Kate's hand exactly at the right moment, and none watching could know that half an hour before these same instruments had been a pile of unwrapped parcels in the reception area.

Slowly, carefully, Richard's skilled fingers replaced the torn flesh over Sophie's slight head. Kate was almost totally occupied with the anaesthetic—Sophie's rapid pulse and frighteningly low blood-pressure were enough to keep her attention unwaveringly on the child's breathing—but she was aware that what Richard was doing was good. This was no makeshift repair that would need plastic surgery to correct when Sophie's condition improved.

Kate's mind was reeling in amazement. She couldn't believe what she was seeing. It was as if a miracle had blown into Corrook, transforming its meagre medical service into state of the art. This was no makeshift theatre—Sophie would get little extra attention if she were in a major teaching hospital. A plastic surgeon would be doing Richard's job, but to Kate's critical eyes the job Richard was doing seemed just as skilful.

Finally the last stitch was in place. Richard carefully applied a compression bandage to the whole area, but the bleeding had slowed to nothing. At last the plasma could begin to do its job.

'We'll cross-match straight away for a transfusion,' Richard said wearily, turning from the table. 'Heaven knows what her haemoglobin level is.'

'It'll still be coming down,' Kate said. She was still concentrating as she reversed the anaesthetic. 'I'll check it now.' She looked up at Richard. 'I'll finish here. Sophie's parents will be going crazy outside.'

'Yeah.' Richard looked down at Sophie and smiled.

'At least I can tell them some good news.' He smiled at the nurses behind the table and then across at Kate. 'Well done, team.'

'Well done yourself,' Kate said softly. 'Sophie's been lucky to have you.'

Richard's eyes met hers and held. 'And you, Dr Harris. We make a good team.' He turned and left the theatre.

An hour later they were free to leave. Sophie was sleeping soundly, blood dripping steadily into her small veins and her blood-pressure gradually rising. Her mother lay beside her on another bed, and two nurses stayed on duty. Alma, their new matron, went home reluctantly.

'I'll be back at seven a.m.,' she told them. 'From here on, it's all systems go.'

'What are the health inspectors going to say about this?' Kate said dubiously as she accompanied Richard out to the car. 'You haven't been given the all-clear to open yet.'

'I'm more worried about what Bert King's going to say,' Richard said ruefully, opening the passenger door for her. 'I promised him he'd be first patient.'

'I wouldn't worry,' Kate reassured him. 'He's Sophie's great-uncle.'

'You don't say.'

'They're an inbred lot around here.' Kate smiled wearily. 'You have to tread very warily until you figure out just who is related to whom.'

'Thanks for the warning.'

They didn't speak on the short drive back to Richard's house. Richard seemed preoccupied, and Kate was just too tired. She couldn't remember ever feeling this tired. It was as if, by taking the burden of responsibility from her shoulders, Richard had allowed her to relax. The big car purred through the night. The upholstery was soft and luxurious. Kate closed her eyes and let herself drift into sleep.

It was a lovely, lovely dream. Warmth, and comfort, and caring. . . Strong arms, lifting, holding, caressing. Deep brown eyes laughing down at her, telling her she was loved. . . Telling her that the long nightmare of loneliness was over. Being carried surely, strongly through the night and then lowered into a soft cocoon of bedclothes. Warmth. . .

And those eyes. . .bending over her, watching her, laughing at her but only with kindness, and with love. . . And then lips softly brushing hers, and whispering goodnight as she drifted blissfully through her dream. . .

CHAPTER SIX

KATE woke to warmth. Weak winter sunlight was streaming in to lie across the big patchwork quilt. The quilt was soft with the lightness of pure down, yet she was so warm. . . She couldn't remember ever having been so warm. . .

Her initial sleepy pleasure faded. Consciousness swept fully back and she sat up with a jolt. She was in a huge oak bed and it wasn't hers. This wasn't her room and it wasn't her house. . .

The memory of the night before came flooding back and her mind recoiled in horror. What on earth had she done? How much had been just a dream?

She stared down at her clothing. No longer was she wearing her serviceable skirt and blouse. She still had on her soft nylon slip and undergarments but that was all. Even her stockings were gone.

'I can't remember getting undressed,' she whispered. 'Surely I wouldn't have let him. . .'

She stared wildly around the neatly ordered bedroom. Her clothes were folded on the big armchair by the door. Kate threw back the bedclothes and then swiftly pulled them up again as heavy footsteps announced she had company.

The door swung open and Richard came in. He was casually dressed in jeans and a checked, open-necked shirt, and he carried a tray. The smell of coffee preceded him.

'Well, well,' he smiled. 'You've decided to wake. Good afternoon.'

Kate clutched her bedclothes to her neck and cast a desperate glance at her wristwatch. Ten a.m. She shook her wrist in disbelief and Richard laughed. He placed the tray on the bedside table and perched easily on the end of the bed.

'It's worrying,' he smiled. 'I'm beginning to think my associate is a sluggard as well as a miser. . .'

Kate flushed. 'I would never. . . I don't. . .'

Richard raised his eyebrows as Kate's usually pale complexion deepened to rose. 'I hope you're not trying to tell me you don't drink coffee,' he said. 'I've just brewed fresh.' He reached over and took two mugs from the tray, handing one to Kate. Kate stared at it, torn between the need to take it and the desperate need to hang on to her bedclothes. Finally she slid down, clutched the quilt with one hand and graciously accepted the coffee with the other. Richard's grin deepened.

'I don't remember ending up here,' Kate said, a little breathlessly.

'You went to sleep,' Richard informed her. 'Sugar? Milk?' He poured milk from a small jug into both mugs.

'In the car?'

'In the car.'

'Then. . . Then how did I get undressed?' Kate's voice wasn't quite steady.

'You're not totally undressed,' Richard said helpfully. He smiled reassuringly down at her. 'It didn't seem worth the effort to go any further.'

Kate's colour went from rose to beetroot. The bedroom seemed suddenly insufferably hot.

'You didn't have to,' she muttered. 'I could have slept in my clothes.' She took a sip of coffee and tasted nothing.

Richard nodded. 'They would have been dreadfully crushed,' he said, in mock-seriousness. 'And even though they're hardly Paris originals, you seem inordinately attached to them. In fact I've hardly seen you in anything else since we arrived. And I was happy to oblige,' he assured her.

'Am I sleeping in your bed?' Kate cut in.

Richard's smile was full of lazy laughter. 'Of course. That's where all my women friends sleep.'

Kate's coffee slipped in her lifeless hands and some splashed on to the counterpane. She bit her lip. 'I. . . I'm sorry. Where. . .where did you sleep?'

'I have a very comfortable settee,' Richard assured her. 'Not like some people I know. . .' He stood up. 'The bacon will be cooked by now. One slice of toast or two, my lady?'

'I. . . None,' Kate managed. 'I have to go home.'

'Not until you've had breakfast,' Richard said firmly. 'To refuse what I've cooked would be the height of bad manners, after all the effort I've gone to.'

'You mean throwing bacon into a pan,' Kate said nastily.

'You don't know the half of it,' he assured her, walking out of the door. 'There's eggs as well.'

Kate was left, staring at the open door. She didn't know whether to laugh or cry.

Three minutes later he was back, striding into the room with laden plates. Once again the smell preceded him, the lovely, rich smell of lightly fried bacon, tomato and eggs. Kate was still in bed. She wanted above all else to be dressed, but Richard had left the door open, and Kate hadn't been game to take the plunge from the bed to the chair. She was stuck.

She took the plate with as much grace as she could muster, and gazed down at it with astonishment. The meal was presented with the air of a professional. The eggs were perfectly fried in gold and white rings, and the crispy bacon lay beside it as a wreath. On the side lay tiny wedged tomatoes and the plate was garnished with slivers of parsley. Toast lay beside the meal, cut into dainty triangles.

'I thought your speciality was TV dinners?' Kate said accusingly.

'I know how to make breakfast look good,' he admitted. 'My mother was ill for some time before she died, and breakfast was really the only proper meal she ate.' His smile slipped a little, and as he stared at his plate Kate knew he was seeing something else.

'How did she die?' she said softly.

'What?' Richard's attention swivelled back and he shrugged. 'Sorry. I didn't mean. . .'

'How did she die?' Kate repeated.

'Emphysema,' he said bluntly. 'And heart disease in the end. A bit like your Miss Souter.' Richard handed her a knife and fork.

'You were fond of her?'

He shrugged. 'She was quite a lady, my mother. When my father died our financial affairs were in a mess. She worked herself to the bone to make sure we didn't go under.'

Kate looked up and her green eyes narrowed. 'Wouldn't she disapprove of the way you're splashing money around now?' she asked quietly.

Richard frowned. 'I'm not splashing money,' he told her. 'I'm investing in the future.'

Kate grimaced. She had heard that line before, over and over.

They ate in silence, both deep in their thoughts. Kate had tucked the top of the sheet into her slip, and she was being very careful. Every now and then she had to put down her knife and fork and carefully readjust her modest arrangement.

'I've heard of table napkins, but this is ridiculous,' Richard said, as she finally finished. 'OK, Miss Prim. You may now slide under the covers and be modest.'

'I'm getting up,' Kate said resentfully. 'I have to go home. And one of us should be down at the hospital to check on Sophie. You may shelve your responsibilities at the weekend, but I don't.'

Richard stood looking down at her for a long moment. His smile slowly faded and his expression was inscrutable. Kate lay back on the pillows, her tangled chestnut curls spread out on the whiteness of the pillow.

'You really have judged me, haven't you, Dr Harris?'

'I just know your type,' Kate threw at him.

Richard carefully placed the plates on the bedside table and sat down again. 'What type am I?' he asked pleasantly.

Kate flushed. This was really the way to endear herself to her new employer, she thought ruefully. And yet. . .what was it about this man that made her want to hurt him—that made her want to drive him away? It was as if she knew that with him she was vulnerable. He looked at her with those damned eyes that saw all the way through. . .

'You don't worry about consequences,' she said stiffly. 'You just do what you want. Like now. I'm grateful for the breakfast but Sophie hasn't seen a doctor for nearly twelve hours.'

Richard drummed his fingers on the counterpane and eyed her speculatively. 'That's where you're wrong, lady,' he said quietly.

'Wr-wrong?' Kate's voice faltered.

'Wrong,' he said decisively. 'As a matter of fact, Sophie's been checked twice. Once at five a.m. when the staff rang me because the bleeding had restarted. It wasn't as bad as they feared. I adjusted the dressing and came back home. And three-quarters of an hour ago, just before you woke, I went down, checked on a still sleeping Sophie, sorted out the nursing roster for the day, rang up Melbourne, had a chat to a plastic surgeon to see if there was any point in sending her on, and then came back here—to make coffee and find you just waking up. I accept your label of spendthrift, but

I'm damned if I'll have you question my professional competence or concern.'

Kate stared up at him in horror. Her hands slipped on the sheet and it fell away. She made a futile clutch at it, but of more concern was the anger she had engendered in those eyes. The laughter was completely gone.

'I'm. . . I'm sorry,' she faltered. 'I didn't know. . .'

'And it's so much easier to judge rather than find out, isn't it, Dr Harris?' Richard said ruthlessly.

'I don't. . . I try not to judge. . .'

'That's nonsense and you know it,' Richard snapped. 'You judged me the moment you met me. And you disapprove. Just because I move fast. . .'

'You don't think things through,' Kate said weakly. 'To set up this medical service on a whim. . .'

Richard shook his head. 'It's not a whim,' he said flatly. 'If you called it a dream then you might be right. It's a dream I've had for years. And when I saw this place open and waiting, I knew the time had come to convert the dream to reality. And you can't judge a man for knowing what he wants. . .'

Kate met his eyes, and the normal laughter had been replaced completely by anger. It was as if he was defying her to challenge him yet again. And she couldn't. She couldn't think of a word to say. His eyes held hers, challenging, and she was close to tears.

'I'm sorry,' she whispered. 'But I don't think. . .'

He put out a hand and touched her lips, lightly holding her mouth closed. 'I don't want to hear what you think any more, Dr Harris. You've insulted me enough for one morning.'

Kate flinched back from his touch. 'I didn't mean to,' she managed.

He stared at her, considering. 'Oh, but I think you did, Dr Harris. I think your insults were deliberate.'

'Why. . .why would I want to insult you?'

Richard's finger was still on her face, tracing the contours of her cheek, and his eyes were still angry. His touch was a taunt. 'Because you're afraid, Dr Harris.'

She knocked his hand away in anger. 'Why would I be afraid of you?' Her voice was a breathless squeak.

His hand moved down, and he traced the hollow of her smooth white throat. 'Because I'm a man who knows what he wants,' he said slowly. 'And I'm starting to suspect I want you. . .'

Kate gasped. She shoved herself backwards in the bed. The sheet was left behind. She clutched at it, but it was held by Richard's weight and didn't follow.

'Well, I don't want you,' she spat. 'I don't want——'

'I don't think you know what you want, Dr Harris,' Richard said politely. 'And I think you should stop making snap judgements.' His hands came behind her to grip her shoulders. She was held, her face locked to his, her flashing eyes glaring up at him. 'I think you should learn, just occasionally, to run with your emotions.'

'Don't be crazy,' she threw at him.

'I can't help it,' he said firmly. 'It's the way you make me feel. Like I either have to slap your lovely face, or kiss it.' He stared at her for a long moment, the anger slowly fading. 'Now what, Dr Harris? What would you have me do?' And he bent and kissed her.

His mouth brooked no denial. His mouth still held the trace of anger — and his anger was seeking a response from her. He was searching for the trace of fire he had felt the night before, and his lips held hers until he found it.

It was there. Kate couldn't deny it. She could fight all she liked with her mind but her body betrayed her. His hands gripped the naked skin of her shoulders and she felt a shudder of pure animal pleasure run through her at the feel of his grip. Her lips opened involuntarily, allowing him to deepen the kiss, to come closer. . .

She was crazy. Her head was screaming it at her, telling her to hit, scratch, get away from this man. She couldn't, she told herself. And yet she knew she could. All she had to do was fight.

She couldn't fight. Not while these hands were holding her, and these lips were searching hers. She felt his tongue run along the white smoothness of her teeth and from a long way away she heard herself give a tiny moan of pleasure.

He was so large. . . She could feel the strength of his hard, muscular body against the sheer fabric of her slip. Her breasts rose and fell with her breathless disarray, and Richard moved suddenly so the firm, rounded swell of them was against him. His hand fell to cup them and his kiss deepened. . .deepened. . .

Kate was beyond reason—beyond anger—beyond any emotion other than primitive need. She had been alone too long. This man set fires alight within her that she'd thought were extinguished forever. He just had to touch her and her body screamed its own response. Oh, God, she wanted him. . . She put her hands up and ran her fingers through the coarse waves of his fair hair. She wanted him closer. . .closer. . .

The soft nylon fabric of her slip was thrust down and her wispy bra disappeared. Richard's hands caressed each breast in turn, and then he stooped to taste the taut nipples with his tongue. Kate's body arched in ecstasy. She gave a sob of pleasure, and of need. . . And suddenly Richard drew back, holding her at arm's length and gazing into her dazed eyes.

'Kate. . .' It was a ragged whisper. With a shock Kate realised that his need was as great as her own. She met his look, drowning in the depths of his dark eyes. Don't stop, her eyes were saying. I want you. . .

'You see,' he whispered, his eyes caressing hers. 'Some things don't have to be considered. Some things just happen, and because they happen fast it doesn't mean they're wrong.'

'You mean. . .' Kate searched desperately for control and found a vestige. Her voice came out a ragged gasp. 'You mean I should let you make love to me. . .'

'It's not me doing all the making,' he teased.

'I don't. . .' Kate's voice broke on a sob. She stared down at twisted sheet. 'Richard, I don't want this.'

'Yes, you do.'

'I don't.' Another tiny sob. 'Please, Richard. . .'

He sat staring down at her, his eyes puzzled. Finally he reached for her hand and held it up. On the third finger of her left hand was a wedding-band. 'Because of this?' he said slowly.

Kate stared at the narrow band of gold. She had left it on even after the divorce was finalised because it protected her from just such a situation as this. At least, it was supposed to. . .

'Yes,' she said slowly. She couldn't think of anything else to say.

'Is he dead?'

'N-no.'

'With someone else?'

'Yes.' Kate flung herself out of the bed and crossed swiftly to the pile of her clothes, unconcerned by her near-naked body. It seemed more important to reach the security of her pile of dowdy clothes. Richard didn't move. He sat watching as she flung on her skirt and blouse, and shoved her feet into her flat slip-on shoes.

'You know, if all you ever wore during your marriage was that skirt, I can't say I blame him,' Richard said drily, laughter edging back into his voice.

'I didn't —— ' Kate said, and then bit her denial back. It was no business of Richard Blair's what she had worn for the duration of her marriage.

'You didn't just wear the skirt.' Richard stood and swiftly crossed the room. Before Kate knew what he was about he had seized her shoulders and swung her around to face him. 'Then the man's a fool.' His voice faded into uncertainty. 'The man's a fool anyway. Wear sackcloth and ashes and you're still very beautiful, Kate.' He stooped to kiss the tiny hollow of her neck. 'But I would so like to see you dressed as you deserve. Satins, silks. . .'

'Something else for you to splash your money on, no doubt,' Kate said waspishly. 'Well, no, thanks. I've no inclination to become your fancy woman.'

'How about my wife?'

Kate gasped. She took a step back and stared at Richard, her mouth falling open. 'How. . .how dare you?'

'How dare I what?' Richard sounded amused.

'How dare you make fun of me?'

'I don't believe I intended to make fun of you,' he said softly. 'A serious offer, Kate. . .'

'W-why?'

'I've told you. I'm a man who knows what he wants. And I want you.'

'Well, I don't want you.' Kate was close to yelling. Her breath was coming in ragged gasps and tears of anger welled in her eyes. 'I've known you less than a week. You storm into this town, you splash money around like water, you buy the affection of the townspeople, do me out of a practice and then propose marriage. . . Is this supposed to be a sop to your conscience?'

'I don't usually appease my conscience by proposing marriage,' Richard smiled. 'It could end up getting very messy if I made a habit of it.'

Kate refused to meet his smile. She was pulling on her coat as if her life depended on it. All she wanted was to get away from this man who was tearing her world apart.

'Kate——'

'Get away from me.' She was crying openly now, trying to control her humiliation but failing miserably. 'Leave me alone. I don't want to be one of your jokes.'

'Kate. . .' His hands came out and gripped her fiercely—possessively. 'Kate, can't you see that I was never further from joking in my life? I'm deadly serious.'

'Then you're quite mad,' she flung at him. 'You don't know me. You met me a week ago and apart from the fact that I have a medical degree you know nothing about me. Nothing!'

'I know nothing,' he said quietly. 'But I know everything I need to know. Kate, you must feel——'

'I don't feel anything,' she sobbed.

'Liar.'

'It's just pure physical attraction,' she managed. 'Just that. And you don't propose marriage on that basis. At least you might if you want your marriage to last for a week, until something better comes along or you discover your true love snores, or spends the housekeeping on the racecourse. . .'

'I wondered when we'd get around to money again,' Richard said conversationally.

Kate flung up her arm and struck his hands from her shoulders. 'I'm going home,' she said savagely. 'I've agreed to work with you for a month, which means I have three more weeks. You have three weeks to find yourself another partner.'

'I have three weeks to change your mind,' he said softly. 'I don't love lightly, Kate.'

'You don't love at all,' she whispered, and turned and fled.

Kate shook all the way home. Her little car was easy to handle on the twisty road, and there was no traffic, which was just as well. She was having trouble steering through the mist of tears filling her eyes.

'Damn him,' she said aloud into the silence. 'How dare he walk into my life and turn it upside-down? What does he expect me to do? Fall into his arms? Swear undying love on less than a week's acquaintance?'

It seemed that was just what he did expect. 'What would he have done if I had fallen into his arms when he proposed?' Kate whispered. 'Married me?' The idea was absurd. Her heart cringed from the thought of such an action. Another marriage. . . With a man who was as big a fool as Doug. . .

He was different from Doug, though. Kate realised with a jolt that Doug had faded. Her vision of the man she had been married to had diminished, and the pain that had dwelt within her for so long, the overriding bitterness, had been replaced.

Replaced by what? By a pair of mocking brown eyes, and hands that were at once gentle and brutally strong. By a man who knew what he wanted the moment he saw it and moved heaven and earth to attain it. . .

'I've gone from the frying-pan straight into the fire,' she said bitterly. 'I should walk out now. I'm mad to stay another three weeks.'

But she had promised. And Richard was paying her salary. There was another instalment due on her parents' mortgage. To walk away without another job would mean the forfeiture of their home.

'I'll just have to put my nose down and work,' Kate said grimly to the silence. 'I have better things to think about than marriage with a fool. . .'

A fool. . . She labelled him and repeated the word over and over in her head, but her heart refused to agree. All her heart could feel was the warmth of laughing brown eyes, and a kiss that was as tender as it was possessive.

CHAPTER SEVEN

KATE spent the rest of her Saturday doing housework. She had done little for weeks, and everywhere she looked there were things needing attention.

Her house was a pretty little cottage. She had loved it on sight, and would dearly like the money to furnish it appropriately. Like Richard's, she thought ruefully.

Why did her thoughts always go back to Richard? She worked hard, trying to drive away the events of the last twenty-four hours with pure physical effort, but his image would not fade.

Finally, towards evening, she ran a deep bath and sank into it with gratitude.

She hadn't indulged in such a luxury for weeks. It was because of the phone, she thought thankfully. Saturday afternoon was usually busy, with injuries from the various local sporting events coming thick and fast. In midwinter the football season was at its height. Corrook fielded three teams, junior, under-eighteens and seniors, and when they played at home Kate often just gave up and went to the match. It was easier than being called back and forth to the club rooms to deal with the myriad minor injuries each match involved.

Not this Saturday, though. Kate looked at her watch as she laid it on the washstand before sliding into the steaming water. The football would be just finishing. Richard had taken the phone, so Richard bore the responsibility. I hope he works his fingers to the bone, she thought savagely. The warm water enfolded her and she closed her eyes in pleasure.

And then opened them. Wide. The football mustn't

have occupied Richard completely. It was his voice
calling from the veranda.

'Kate? Can I come in?'

Kate gasped and looked wildly round for her towel.
It was on the hook on the back of the door. She stood
up, dripping, leaned over and grabbed. Her foot slipped
on the soapy porcelain and she fell heavily forward.
Her foot slid out and twisted. The ligaments in her
ankle tore as she went down and she ended in a forlorn,
sodden heap on the floor.

She didn't think she cried out, but she must have.
The pain in her ankle stabbed like fire. She struggled to
rise but the pain caught her again and held. She sank
back, biting her lip in agony.

'Kate?' Richard's voice had risen in concern. 'What's
wrong?'

'Go away,' she called weakly, wincing as the pain
gripped her. She clutched her ankle and fought to get
her voice back to normal. 'Go away.'

'What the hell. . .?' She could hear the concern in
his voice, and she heard the front door opening. 'Where
are you?'

'I'm having a bath,' Kate said tightly.

'And someone's sticking knives into you while you
do, I suppose,' Richard responded. His voice sounded
closer. 'Where are you?'

'I'm in the bathroom.' Kate was gripping her ankle
and trying desperately not to let the pain sound in her
voice. 'Where else would I be having a bath?'

'What's wrong, Kate?'

'There's nothing wrong.' Her voice was rising as he
came closer. 'There's nothing wrong, Richard Blair.
Leave me alone.' The bare linoleum floor was cold on
her naked skin and the shock of the fall was making her
tremble. The towel hung high on the hook, out of her
reach. And then the door-handle moved downwards
and Richard Blair walked into the bathroom.

He stopped short at what he saw, the naked girl huddled painfully on the floor, and then he moved forward swiftly. 'Kate——'

'Get out of here,' she shouted. 'You did this. . . Get out!'

'What did I do?' He turned to look for the towel, lifted the threadbare piece of towelling from the hook behind the door and rejected it. Throwing it aside, he bent over Kate. 'Have you hurt your back?'

'No.' She was cringing away from him, mortified and in pain. 'I've twisted my ankle. Please, Richard, just leave me alone.'

She was ignored. His fingers were on the wet skin of her ankle, gently touching. 'Not just twisted. It's sprained or broken,' he said grimly. 'It's coming up beautifully. And so are you, Kate, my girl.' With one easy movement he caught the dripping Kate in his arms and lifted her from the floor.

'Put me down.' Kate was crying in humiliation and rage. She formed her hands into fists and crashed them against his chest. 'Put me down, damn you.'

'I'll put you down when I find somewhere a bit more comfortable than the floor,' he assured her, taking her back out into the living-room. 'For heaven's sake, woman, you're freezing.'

Kate gave a moan of despair. This couldn't be happening to her. What had happened to the cool professionalism of Dr Kate Harris? She felt about as professional as a six-year-old.

Richard looked at the settee and rejected it with one swift glance. It was vinyl, hard and unyielding. With his sodden burden still in his arms he kicked open the bedroom door and took Kate through. He laid her gently on the bed, and Kate made a grab for the modesty of a blanket.

'I'd dry yourself first,' Richard told her. 'If you wet the bedding you'll never get it dry, especially in this place. Why on earth don't you light a fire?' He walked swiftly out, grabbed the threadbare towel from the bathroom and brought it in again, eying it in distaste. Kate grabbed it, but the sudden movement caused her to whimper in pain. Richard's eyes narrowed.

'That bad?' Then, as she didn't answer he bent to look and gently examine. Her left ankle was swelling alarmingly.

He looked up at her face, noting the pain behind the anger in her eyes. She was clutching the towel across her, striving for some vestige of modesty.

'OK, my love,' he said softly. 'Let's get you dry and warm before we worry about the ankle.'

'I am not your love,' she spat.

'No,' he said equably. 'For now you are not my love. You are my patient. And there is no other doctor in the valley so you have no choice, Dr Harris. Lie still or I'll call the ambulance and have Joe take you to Melbourne.'

'Don't be ridiculous.' Shards of pain were coursing through her from her ankle and she was having trouble getting any words out at all. 'I'll be all right. I just want to be left alone.'

'But you accused me of causing this,' Richard said evenly. He took the towel from her lifeless fingers and started rubbing the remaining moisture from her body. 'So what is a man to do? Desert you in your hour of need?' He smiled down at her and his brown eyes were understanding. 'Lie still, my Kate, and let me help.'

It seemed there was no option. She lay back helplessly on the pillows while Richard towelled her dry. His hands ran over the smooth contours of her body with easy competence. With anyone else Kate could have blocked it out as being the actions of a professional carer doing his job. But it was Richard. . .

Why was he different? Why should his touch make her body shudder in response? The pain in her ankle receded as he gently stroked her dry. His strong, competent hands followed the lines of her body and her body ached to his touch.

Finally she was dry, rubbed to warmth. The awful tremors ceased. Richard pulled the big, woollen blanket around her and then left her. A moment later he was back, carrying her battered case.

'I've been using your equipment all day.' He smiled at her. 'And you paid for it. You'll have to send me a bill. At least now I can use some of it on you.' He laid it on the bedside table and opened it. 'Morphine?'

'It's not bad enough for morphine,' Kate said tightly. She held the big blanket around herself.

'It's bad enough for something,' Richard said evenly. 'You're as white as a sheet.' He went to the foot of the bed and lifted the blanket from her ankle, grimacing at what he saw. 'You've made a mess of this. Why on earth don't you have a non-slip pad in your bath?'

'I don't usually slide,' Kate told him. 'Only when I panic. . .'

'And I made you panic.' Richard nodded. 'I can see that. There's a lot in me to make maidens panic.' He was fingering the ankle gently, watching her face. 'Non-slip pads are essential in any bath, and not just for small children and old people. I had a patient in England—a boy of sixteen—who turned himself into a paraplegic after a bath accident.'

'Your bedside manner is so reassuring,' Kate snapped. 'Lecture on foolishness to stupid patient. All right. I know I should have had a bath mat. But. . .'

'You couldn't afford one,' Richard supplied helpfully. He frowned down at her foot. 'Kate, we're going to have to take X-rays.'

'It's not broken,' Kate said abruptly. 'I would have heard it break.'

'You can't tell,' he told her. 'There's enough swelling to disguise a fracture, and you've sure as hell damaged the ligaments.' He reached into the case and retrieved a wide elastic bandage, and for the next couple of minutes there was silence while he skilfully strapped her ankle. Finally he had done all he could. He looked around the room. 'Do you own anything to wear except for that awful damned skirt?'

'I. . . There's a tracksuit in my wardrobe,' Kate told him. 'But I'm not going to the city for X-rays.'

'You don't have to. I've an X-ray machine at the hospital.'

'I might have known,' Kate said crossly. 'CT scanner as well?'

CT scanners—machines capable of neurological X-rays—ran into millions of dollars, and only the major city hospitals owned them. Richard grinned. 'Not quite yet,' he admitted. 'Even I might have to save for a week or so before I purchase one of those. But I certainly have a machine which will check this foot. Now, clothes. Dr Harris. I'm not taking you naked.' He grinned. 'I have some idea of modesty, even if you don't.'

As he failed to elicit an answer he crossed to the wardrobe. 'Wow, what a choice,' he told Kate as he inspected the contents. 'You really are set for the high life.'

Kate flushed. She hadn't spent any money on clothes since Doug had left, and when she had moved to Corrook she had left any dressier clothes with her parents. There seemed no point in bringing them. 'Just get me my tracksuit,' she said bitterly. 'I might not be able to stop you seeing what's none of your concern, but if you were a gentleman. . .'

'Oh, but I'm not.' He smiled across at her. He pulled a warm crimson tracksuit from the hanger and carried it across to the bed. 'If I were a gentleman I'd be on the other side of the door right now, while you struggled painfully to dress yourself. Instead of which, I have every intention of assisting you.'

'I can dress myself.' Kate sat up and made a grab for her tracksuit and then gave an involuntary gasp of pain.

'Kate.' Richard's hands held her shoulders, and he pushed her firmly backwards. 'I came by your house to take you down to the hospital because I wish to check Sophie's wound, and I want another doctor present when I remove the pressure bandage. I still need you, damaged ankle and all. All you're doing now is wasting my time. Now, let me help you into your tracksuit, or I'll pick you up in your blanket and take you to the hospital as you are.'

Kate drew in her breath sharply. 'You wouldn't dare.'

'Try me,' he said sternly. He held out the top of her tracksuit. 'Submit or face the consequences.'

Kate stared up at him. His mouth was stern but a tiny demon of laughter lurked in the back of his eyes. She desperately wanted to defy him, but couldn't think how. Her foot was a grinding ache, and she was close to tears. She held out her arms.

'All right,' she said bitterly. 'I accept your oh, so gracious offer of help.'

'Very wise,' Richard said.

Ten minutes later she was ensconced in the back seat of the Mercedes. 'You'll be more comfortable with your foot up,' Richard told her. He had given her an injection for the pain, but it was still aching dully.

'I can't believe I've done this,' Kate muttered between clenched teeth. 'Of all the dreadful weeks. . .'

'Come now,' Richard chided her. 'It hasn't been all bad. A new hospital. . .a fantastically competent new partner. . .'

'And modest,' Kate said savagely. 'You forgot to say modest.'

'And modest,' Richard grinned. He was driving carefully down the rough track, mindful of the pain undue jolting would cause the girl on the back seat. 'I don't usually forget to include that on my curriculum vitae.'

Kate bit her lip and said nothing. Rather to her surprise, Richard also fell silent. It was as if he knew that Kate was very close to her limit. Her world was being torn apart and she was adrift, in a limbo she didn't understand. Her damaged ankle was symbolic of a deeper instability, she thought fearfully. The world she had tried so hard to control was spinning crazily about her. And it was all because of this man. . .

She shifted on the seat and pain stabbed yet again through the ankle. Concentrate on the pain, she told herself grimly. At least it's real. At least it has substance. . .

As Richard Blair did not? She looked up at his broad back, in the seat in front of her. He certainly seemed to have substance — there was so much of him. But the man was mad. Crazy! An impetuous fool who would be gone as soon as his money ran out, no doubt leaving a trail of debts behind him.

'I won't, you know,' he said casually.

'Won't. . .won't what?'

'Won't walk out.'

Kate drew in her breath. 'I never said you would.'

'You don't have to,' he told her, without turning. He was concentrating on the road. 'I can hear it every time you open your mouth. I can see it in the way you look at me. You don't trust me.'

'Why should I?' The words were out before she had a chance to consider and Kate bit her lip in dismay. She hadn't meant to be so blunt.

'Because you're in love with me.'

Once again Kate drew in her breath, but this time she didn't speak. She couldn't.

'I'm right, aren't I, Dr Harris?' Richard said cheerfully as they rounded the next bend.

'No!' It was a gasp.

'Hmm.' Richard turned his head momentarily and flashed her a smile. 'I could have sworn you're afraid of me, Dr Harris, and I can't think of a more logical reason for your fear.'

'I'm not. . . I'm not afraid of you.' Kate fought for breath. Her voice, when she finally spoke, was icy. 'And I don't love you, Dr Blair, regardless of how puffed up you are in your own conceit. I don't even like you. You stand for everything I most dislike, and I'll walk away from here in three weeks with not a backward glance.'

'Hobble away if that ankle's broken,' Richard said softly.

Kate's fingernails clenched into her palms. She wanted something to throw. Richard had placed a pillow behind her, but the imprudence of throwing it at the driver of a moving car was enough to penetrate her almost stammering rage.

'You can throw it as soon as the car stops,' Richard said soothingly. 'If it's only the pillow I promise not even to duck.'

'You. . .' Words failed her. Kate sank into furious silence. Her anger made her even forget the pain of her ankle. She lay rigid, her lips clenched tightly closed until the car swung into the hospital car park.

Richard pulled the car to a halt before the main door of the hospital. As he opened the back door, Kate finally found her voice.

'You don't have to lift me.'

Richard looked sardonically down. 'Are you proposing to walk?'

'If this is any sort of hospital it'll have a trolley,' Kate snapped. 'Or don't your millions extend to cover necessities?'

Richard looked down at her, his eyes expressionless. Then, slowly, he raised his hand in a mock-salute.

'Your wish is my command, Dr Harris.' He wheeled round and entered the hospital, leaving her fuming on the back seat of the car.

Two minutes later he was back, but not alone. He was wheeling a large, gleaming aluminium trolley made up with soft mattress and bedding, and a nurse walked at either side.

'We're a little short-handed, Dr Harris,' Richard said pleasantly. 'Our orderlies don't start work until Monday. But we'll do our best.' He motioned to the bemused nurses. 'Shall we?'

Before she knew it, Kate had been lifted competently from the car by their several hands, and had been laid on the trolley with minimal movement. She tried to sit up but Richard's hands held her shoulders inexorably down.

'Lift the rail, Sister,' he said briefly. 'We don't want our patient rolling off.'

'Will you let me alone?' Kate fought futiley against Richard's hands. 'For heaven's sake, I've only twisted an ankle.'

'I did think that,' Richard said solemnly. 'A sore ankle hardly warranted this treatment, but a trolley you ordered, and a trolley you shall have.' He motioned to the nurse at the head of the trolley. 'Lead on, Sister. We have our second patient.'

There was nothing for Kate to do but lie back and fume.

Much to her relief, the X-ray showed no fracture. Richard held it up to the light and considered.

'You've been lucky,' he told her. 'You'll be on crutches for a couple of weeks, though.'

'You'd better find another associate immediately, then,' Kate said bitterly. 'A disabled doctor is little use to you.'

He looked at her for a long moment. She was still

lying on the trolley, a blanket covering the crimson tracksuit. Her eyes were still too big for her lovely face, and her skin was white with shock and strain.

'It won't hurt me to take most of the load for the next couple of weeks,' he said firmly. 'I need you for advice, and as of Monday we'll open the surgery. You can sit behind a desk dispensing advice and prescriptions while I run my legs off doing the house calls.'

'And then just as I recover I leave,' Kate said bitterly. 'That's hardly fair.'

'Fair's for me to judge,' she was told firmly. 'I'm your employer.' He stood silently for a moment. 'Kate, I still need to check Sophie. If any of the reattached tissue hasn't taken, it'll need to be trimmed, and I won't do that without an anaesthetist on hand.' He frowned. 'Are you up to sitting in a chair in Theatre while I check?'

Kate's eyes flew up to him. He really did surprise her. She judged him harshly, but of his competence and concern for his patient there seemed little doubt. Another doctor might have left the check for the morning. The chances of dead tissue needing to be trimmed now were slim, Kate knew. However, with a wound across the little girl's forehead, the scarring from not catching it immediately would be considerable. She nodded.

'I can cope,' she said.

Richard nodded as though he had expected nothing less. 'I'll find a wheelchair,' he said. 'I know you're inordinately fond of your trolley, but it's a little difficult to administer an anaesthetic while supine.'

Much to Kate's relief, Sophie's wound did not require trimming. The child lay big-eyed while Richard carefully checked the dressing. She was still heavily sedated, but she was awake.

'It's a bit sore,' she said sleepily as Richard reapplied the pressure bandage.

'It will be for a while,' Richard told her. 'You have a mighty cut. Fifty-seven stitches!'

'Fifty-seven. . .' Despite her pain and drowsiness Sophie was pleased. 'Mike Crimshaw—he's another kid in grade five—cut his arm open on a broken bottle and only had twenty-five. And that was a huge cut.'

'He'll have to do better than that to beat you,' Richard promised.

'Fifty-seven. . .' Sophie was drifting into sleep as Richard's examination ended. 'And Mum says I'm the first person for ages to be in this hospital, and I'm the only patient. . .' On this note of profound satisfaction she closed her eyes.

Richard finished adjusting the dressing and then signalled the night sister to wheel Sophie back to the ward.

'It's starting to seem like a real hospital,' Kate said slowly.

'What do you mean, woman?' Richard demanded. 'It is a real hospital. It has a staff of five nurses, two doctors and two patients. Even if one of us is playing a dual role.'

'What do you mean?' Kate asked suspiciously.

Richard wheeled Kate over to the basins, and set her chair where she could wash. 'It means, Dr Harris, that you're both doctor and patient. You'll not go home tonight with your ankle like that.'

'Don't be ridiculous,' Kate said, startled. 'Of course I'm going home.'

'How?' Richard finished washing and turned to lean against the sink, facing the girl in the wheelchair. He folded his arms and waited.

Kate flushed. 'I'll call Pete if you won't drive me,' she said stiffly. 'He'll take me in his taxi.'

'And you'll prepare yourself a three-course meal when you get there, I suppose,' Richard said drily.

'And then go for a brisk walk around the top paddock before bed. Don't be silly, Kate. This is the only place for you tonight and you know it. Besides,' he went on relentlessly as he saw her open her mouth to argue, 'I was up most of last night. I had the devil of a job sleeping on that settee and I want to sleep tonight. With you here you can be on call for Sophie.'

'Sophie will sleep through tonight,' Kate retorted.

'You can't be sure of that,' Richard told her. 'And I'm your boss now, Dr Harris. What I say goes, if you want to stay employed for the next three weeks.' He surveyed her thoughtfully. 'And, no matter how angry you are, that seems to be important to you.'

'I need the money,' Kate admitted. 'Otherwise I'd be out of here so fast you wouldn't see me for dust.'

'Now there's a dedicated doctor for you.' Richard's eyes were on Kate's face. 'Just lucky you're beautiful.'

'Oh, shut up,' Kate flung at him. She shoved the wheels of her chair and the chair leapt forward. Instead of turning slowly as she wished, however, the chair responded instantaneously to her vicious tug, and she caught the side of the stainless-steel sink on her arm. She swore and tried to back off. Richard was before her.

'Temper,' he said mildly. 'Just because Dr Blair knows best.'

'Dr Blair does not know best.' Kate's precarious hold on her temper snapped. 'If I were a man I'd punch you so hard. . .'

'Don't let your sex stop you,' Richard said softly, goadingly. He dropped to a crouch before her chair. 'Go ahead, Dr Harris. Slug.'

Kate stared. 'Don't be. . .'

'Don't be what?' The teasing eyes were implacable. 'You want to hit me? Go ahead, Dr Harris. Hit me.'

Once again Kate shoved with her chair, but Richard was firmly in the way. His hands reached out and held the chair. He had dressed in drab green theatre garments for the procedure, and his shock of fair hair and deep brown eyes were startling against it. His hands on the sides of her chair were large and muscled. Kate pushed the chair but it didn't move an inch.

'You're going to have to hit me, Dr Harris,' he said softly. 'It's the only way to move me. And you really want to.'

'I wouldn't give you the pleasure of demeaning myself,' Kate hissed.

'You're beautiful, Kate.'

'I hate you. . .'

Richard shook his head. 'No,' he said slowly. 'You don't, my Kate.' He smiled at her, his slow, heart-stopping smile that made Kate's heart twist within her. 'What's between us isn't hate.'

'Speak for yourself.' Kate's voice had sunk to as low as Richard's and her breath was coming in angry gasps. 'You know nothing about me. Nothing.'

'I know everything I need to know.'

'You're mad.'

'You keep saying that.' He grinned. 'No doubt one day you'll be proved right.' He placed a finger on her flushed cheek. 'But I'm not mad yet.'

'Doctor. . .'

A voice from the hallway made them both start. Kate flinched but Richard looked calmly around. 'Yes, Sister?'

'The bed for Dr Harris is ready.' The nurse looked nervously from one doctor to the other. 'If she wants it.'

'She wants it.' Richard straightened and took the back handles of Kate's chair, pushing her smoothly forward. 'Bed for you, my girl. A top up of that painkiller, and something to make you sleep, I think.'

'I thought you said you wanted me on call for Sophie,' Kate snapped.

'But you assured me she'd sleep through,' Richard told her. 'And as I'm mad you must surely be the doctor to be believed.'

CHAPTER EIGHT

KATE slept for fifteen hours straight. The combination of the stress of the day before and the pain-killers she had taken took their toll and her exhausted body reacted accordingly. She woke to sun streaming in her neat little hospital room, shining off the newly painted walls and making the metal of her hospital bed gleam.

The bedside clock showed nine o'clock. Kate stirred on her pillows, wincing slightly as she moved her ankle. A cradle protected it from the weight of the bedclothes but it was still painful.

She lay, half in and out of sleep, savouring the lack of urgency. It was Sunday, she was in hospital and Richard was in charge. The outside world could take care of itself today.

A few minutes later the door opened to admit Alma, their matron. She peeped around the door and beamed as she saw Kate was awake.

'Dr Blair said you weren't to be disturbed for anything short of an earthquake,' she smiled. Then, as another face appeared behind her, she turned to the junior nurse. 'Dr Harris needs her breakfast. And afterwards we'll give her a blanket wash.'

Kate's eyes widened and she pushed herself up on the pillows. 'I can take a shower,' she protested.

'I know you can.' Alma smoothed her starched white uniform and crossed to the bed. 'But Dr Blair says you're to have total bed-rest for twenty-four hours, and, to be honest, I'd like the staff to have the practice.' She smiled ruefully. 'We're all a trifle rusty.'

'You didn't seem rusty in Theatre on Friday night,' Kate told the older woman.

'Oh, well. . .' Alma gestured dismissively. 'It comes flooding back.' Her smile deepened. 'And it's so good to be working again. . .' She crossed to plump Kate's pillows. 'Two patients already. And Bert King is coming back tomorrow.'

'We haven't Health Department approval yet,' Kate warned.

'I don't see how they can withhold it now,' Matron said indignantly. 'After all our work. And with our nice Dr Blair in charge. . .'

'Bulldozing all before him,' Kate finished for her. She looked around. 'Where are my clothes?'

Alma looked uneasy. 'Dr Blair took them,' she said.

'He what?'

'He took them with him. He said you'd want something clean to wear going home.'

'I only put the tracksuit on last night,' Kate said, her voice filled with foreboding. 'It was hardly dirty. When does he propose returning?'

'He's already been in this morning,' Alma said. 'He may well pop in this evening, though, especially if we need him.'

'We need him,' Kate said through gritted teeth. 'And we need him before this evening. I want to go home now.'

'Dr Blair's ordered a full day's bed-rest for you,' Matron told her. 'And he said we weren't to take any argument.' She laid a hand placatingly on Kate's shoulder. 'Honestly, dear, you've been working much too hard for so long. Why not give your poor body the rest it deserves?'

'Because Dr Blair ordered me to,' Kate managed. 'And I don't do what that man orders.'

'He's a very ordering sort of person,' the matron smiled. 'And used to having his own way, I suspect.'

'Too much,' Kate said shortly. She threw back the covers, to reveal her skimpy hospital gown. 'Can you contact the taxi service and ask Pete to collect me?' she continued. 'And find me something to wear?'

Alma spread her hands. 'It's more than my job's worth,' she said helplessly. 'Besides, I don't have anything. And your hospital gown is hardly modest.'

Kate swore.

'You know, if I were you I'd just lie back and relax,' Alma said kindly. 'Dr Blair is only doing this for your own good. That's a nasty sprain.'

Kate sank back on to the pillows and glared. 'I don't seem to have much choice,' she said bitterly. 'The man's an autocratic. . .' Words failed her.

'Yes, dear,' Alma said placidly. 'Now, what would you like for breakfast?'

Despite her frustration, the day of enforced rest did Kate more good than she cared to admit. She took strong pain-killers for her ankle, and spent the day drifting in and out of sleep. She was hardly disturbed. The joy of a small country hospital, Kate thought sleepily, was that it could accommodate its routine to its patients. It wasn't imperative that she be woken at six a.m. for a blanket bath before breakfast at seven. If she was asleep, she could be left asleep.

Her tiny hospital room faced north and the weak winter sun soothed and warmed her. Outside, the massive gums surrounding the hospital filtered the light, making the dappled sunlight dance on her white counterpane. She was warm, she was practically pain-free and she slept.

Towards evening she roused to find a pile of glossy magazines on her bedside table. 'I popped home at lunchtime to collect them for you,' Alma smiled when Kate questioned her. 'Our reading material isn't exactly extensive yet.'

'You didn't think of bringing me in something to wear?' Kate asked directly.

'Oh, no, dear.' Alma was shocked. 'What would Dr Blair say?'

What indeed? Kate lay back, baffled, and picked up a magazine. She was still fuzzy with sleep, warm and filled with the luxurious feeling of being pampered. It was hard to be angry.

'How's Sophie?' she asked.

'She's doing beautifully,' Alma beamed. 'Her haemoglobin levels were still very much down so Dr Blair ran a full transfusion — we had to call in blood donors because we don't have supplies yet. Luckily Sophie's O positive, and with such a common group we didn't have any problem. She's been eating, and playing a little Monopoly with her mum. Oh, and she's complaining that her head is itching. If that's all she can find to complain about she'll have no worries.'

'She was lucky,' Kate said slowly.

'She was,' Alma said firmly. 'To have two competent doctors on hand. . .'

'I know,' Kate nodded. 'If it had happened while I was on my own I wouldn't have been able to resew. And whether she would have died from blood-loss on the way to the city. . .' She paused. 'It doesn't bear thinking of.'

'The whole town is lucky,' Alma smiled. 'To have Dr Blair put in so much. . . The town can talk of nothing else. I don't think there's a person in the town who could deny him anything.'

Kate's lips compressed. If these plans caved in. . . 'I just hope the man's done his sums right,' she said slowly. 'It would be dreadful if anything happened now.'

'Why, what could happen?' Alma demanded. 'If the Health Commission refuses to license the place tomorrow I think they'll be tarred and feathered before they leave town. Besides, they've no grounds for refusing.' She motioned out of the window to where a burly

farmer was carting rubbish across the darkening garden.
'The town's put everything into this. Dr Blair didn't
have to ask, but straight after this morning's milking
every able-bodied man and woman in the district turned
up to do the garden. It's been transformed from a
jungle into the most manicured hospital garden from
here to Melbourne.'

Kate smiled but her smile was still doubtful. Richard
Blair was raising such hopes. If they were to be dashed
again as he ran out of money. . .

'Our Dr Harris has no faith.' A rich, deep voice
sounded from the doorway and the matron swung to
face Richard Blair. He was dressed for manual work,
in grubby jeans and a sweat-stained open-necked shirt.
Clearly he had been assisting the working party in the
grounds.

'Oh, Doctor. . .' Matron was blushing like a schoolgirl and Kate shook her head in disbelief. This man had
the whole town at his feet. 'I didn't hear you come in.
Was Sister in the office? I wouldn't have you do a
round unattended.' Clearly Matron's sense of propriety
had been offended by the sight of a doctor finding
patients by himself.

'I think I can manage a ward-round of two by myself,'
Richard smiled. 'I'm hardly likely to forget my instructions before I return to Sister's station. Besides, I'm not
working at the moment.' He looked ruefully down at
his stained work clothes. 'I'm on a social visit.'

He crossed to the bed and looked down, his smile
deepening. Once again, Kate's heart did a crazy jump.
I'm as bad as Matron, she thought crossly, and glared
up at him.

'Did you bring my clothes?'

'No.'

Kate drew in her breath. Behind Richard, Matron
gave an apologetic cough.

'If you want me, just ring the bell, Dr Blair,' she said

softly. 'I. . . I've the medicine trolley to prepare.' She slipped out and Kate stared after her.

'I thought Matron's job was to accompany the doctor,' she said bitterly. 'Not abandon patients to your tender mercy.'

'I told you—it's a social visit,' Richard told her. 'Besides, I think Matron senses a domestic.' He smiled. 'She's a canny soul.'

'A domestic. . .'

'A quarrel between lovers,' Richard explained kindly.

'This is not. . .' Kate's voice was practically a squeak.

'Your clothes will be delivered in the morning,' Richard said solemnly, cutting short her protests. 'Meanwhile, I'm pleased to see those shadows fading.' He touched the soft skin under her eyes. 'I thought they would,' he said in satisfaction.

'And you're always right,' Kate said bitterly. 'Mr Wonderful. The whole town's eating out of your hand.'

'What's wrong with that?' Richard looked out to the grounds beyond Kate's window. The last of the rubbish from the overgrown garden was now a glowing bonfire at the road's edge. 'They have themselves a hospital. Who's gaining, Kate? Me—or the town?'

'Until you run out of money,' Kate said bitterly.

'This place will pay for itself,' Richard told her. He perched himself on the end of her bed, carefully avoiding the cradle.

'When?' Kate shook her head. 'Two patients are hardly going to cover the first week's expenses. I don't know your source of credit. . .'

'What makes you think I'm doing this on credit?'

'I know how much this is worth,' Kate snapped. 'One man couldn't afford all this. Not on a doctor's income.'

'So I must be placing myself deeply in debt,' Richard said slowly. 'And that makes me some sort of a criminal?'

'Yes. . . No. . .' Kate closed her eyes in confusion and weariness. Her ankle was starting to hurt again and she was close to tears. All she wanted was for this overbearing male to leave her be — to get out of her life.

It seemed he had no intention of even leaving her room. When finally she reopened her eyes Richard was still there.

'Do you want to tell me about it, Kate?' he asked gently. 'What has life dished out to you to make you distrust it?'

'I don't distrust life.'

He raised his eyebrows. 'You certainly make a good show of it,' he told her. 'Life hasn't been fun for a long time, has it, Dr Harris?'

'Life isn't fun,' Kate said bitterly. 'But I don't distrust it. I distrust you.'

'Because I threaten you.'

'You don't just threaten me,' Kate said, forcing the words out. 'You threaten the happiness of this town. You take over my livelihood, you make promises to the people of this valley which you must know are air dreams — you live in a soap bubble. And when it bursts you'll walk away and other people will be hurt — not you.'

'Is that what your husband did to you?'

'What my husband did is none of your business.'

'It is my business,' he said softly. He picked up her hand and studied the band of gold. 'You're still hurting because of him, and you're my patient. Anything that hurts you is my business.'

'You look after my ankle,' Kate muttered savagely. 'Nothing else is your concern. And if you weren't the only doctor in town I wouldn't even let you take care of that.'

'How's that for professional trust?' Richard smiled. He bent and kissed her lightly on the lips. 'Katy Harris,

I mean to get around that barrier of suspicion and coldness you've built up so carefully around you. There's a lovely, laughing girl in there, and I mean to rescue her. You'd better draw in your reserves, my love, because I have resources you've yet to dream of. It's a siege, and the attacker has one huge advantge.'

'What. . .?' Kate put her hand to her lips, her cheeks burning. 'What's that?'

'The lovely, laughing Kate really wants to come out. She really wants to love again, and expose her heart to whatever may happen. All I have to do is wait.'

'You know nothing. . .'

'I know you.'

Kate drew in her breath. In frustration her hand reached for her pillow and she swung the soft white foam hard at Richard's head. It caught him full on the face and in its turn was caught itself. Richard took the pillow in one hand and Kate's wrist in another.

'You'll have to find better weapons than that, my Kate,' he warned. 'There's not a lot of mortal blows struck with pillows.'

'I hate you,' Kate stammered through gritted teeth. 'I wish I'd never set eyes on you. You are an obnoxious, conceited toad. . .'

'At least I've made an impression.' He grinned down at her and lightly dropped the pillow back into place. 'Sleep well, my love. I'll see you in the morning.'

'Richard Blair. . .' Oblivious to the nursing staff, Kate's yell sounded down the corridor. 'Richard Blair, where are my clothes?'

Somewhat to her surprise Kate slept well again that night. Her body was catching up on the rest she had denied it for months. It was not until her nose caught the smell of fried bacon drifting down the corridor that she opened her eyes.

'Mmm.' Her nose had not mistaken. Ten seconds

later, Alma appeared around the door bearing a loaded plate.

'I'm sorry to wake you, dear,' she said apologetically. 'But today we have to be spruce.'

'Spruce,' Kate said blankly.

'For the inspection,' the matron explained. She looked nervously at her wristwatch. 'It's at nine o'clock. In half an hour.'

'Half an hour!' Kate's eyes widened. She pushed herself up as Alma manouevred the wheeled tray into position with Kate's breakfast. 'I have to be out of here by then.'

'Nonsense,' Alma said reassuringly. 'It won't hurt the inspection team to see two patients. It'll make us seem more needed.'

'The hospital shouldn't even have one patient,' Kate said brusquely. 'Much less two. . .'

'How could we not treat Sophie?' the matron said. 'You know she would have died if the hospital wasn't here. The inspection team should know that.'

'That's fine, but not me,' Kate said. 'I've only a bad sprain. What possible justification can Richard Blair have for admitting me to an unregistered hospital?'

'I guess we'll have to leave the explaining to Dr Blair,' Matron said trustingly. 'I'm sure he'll have thought of something.'

'He wouldn't have thought of bringing in my clothes?' Kate demanded, her voice holding little hope.

'Well, no, dear. I expect he's been too busy,' Matron soothed. 'Now you finish your breakfast and we'll give your room a good going-over. Nice efficient hospital corners if we're to be inspected.' She bustled off, leaving Kate to fume.

She didn't have to fume very long. At two minutes past nine the sounds in the corridor outside announced the arrival of the Health Commission team of inspection.

From where Kate lay she could hear everything. Voices were raised in protest as Richard and Alma led the team through the hospital. The hospital had no right to be operating, members of the team variously expounded. It broke every rule in the book. Richard deserved to have his licence revoked even before it was issued. Most irregular, was the feeling. Most irregular. And then Richard led them through to Sophie's room.

Sophie's ward was directly opposite Kate's smaller room. Kate listened to the team coming down the corridor, their voices concerned and holding a hint of anger. She heard them walk into Sophie's room and she heard their protests die away.

There were doctors on the inspection panel. They knew, as Richard described the extent of Sophie's injuries, that the tiny hospital had been Sophie's only hope of life.

Sophie helped enormously. Kate, lying back on her pillows, listened to the weak little voice and smiled in appreciation. Sophie had an audience and she was playing it up to the full.

'I would have died,' she said in a thread of a voice, and Kate could just imagine the wan little face wreathed in white bandages lying back against the stark whiteness of the pillows. 'My hair was all pulled off. Just like the Indians, you know,' she informed them proudly. 'Dad says I must be the only kid in all of Australia who knows what it's like to be scalped. If it wasn't for Dr Blair and Dr Harris I'd be pushing up daisies.'

'Sophie!' Sophie's mother, who had hardly left the hospital since her daughter was admitted, raised her voice in expostulation.

'It's true, Mum,' Sophie told her seriously. 'Everyone says. I was really lucky Dr Blair had the hospital ready when he did and there were two doctors.'

The team of inspectors were silenced, each unable to tell Sophie that Richard had no right to open the

hospital for the trivial purpose of saving a life. Finally
one of the team members cleared her throat.

'Is Dr Harris in the hospital?' she asked. 'It was one
of the stipulations that two doctors were available.'

'She's at the surgery,' Richard said briefly. 'This town
can't spare both its doctors at once. I have no idea how
she managed alone for so long. You'll meet her later.'

Kate frowned. Didn't he intend to bring the inspectors into her room?

It seemed he did. Five minutes later her door was
opened and the inspectors filed in. Kate drew her
bedclothes up to her nose and stared.

'Two patients,' one of the inspectors said, his voice
rich with disapproval.

'It never rains but it pours,' Richard said, shaking his
head sadly. 'And with the hospital opened, how could I
refuse this young lady?'

One of the women in the inspection panel picked up
the chart from the end of the bed and read. 'Sprained
ankle?' she read in amazement. Her voice registered
stunned disapproval.

Richard nodded, without comment. He stood
between Kate and the inspection panel as if he was
worried about his patient's reaction to so many people.
'I'll talk about this patient outside if you don't mind,
please.' He motioned meaningfully to the door.

A minute later they were gone. Richard ushered the
last one out, threw a wink at Kate and closed the door
behind them. They walked a few paces down the
corridor before Richard started to talk. With no hesitation Kate scrambled out of bed, hopped awkwardly
to the door and opened it a crack. Richard's lowered
voice carried clearly down the corridor.

'It's not just a sprained ankle,' he explained to the
bemused team members. 'The young lady was found on
Saturday night naked and freezing. She'd slipped in the
bath, I gather, but the actual damage to her ankle is

only a tiny part of her problem. Poor girl. . . She lives alone and hasn't even enough money for a fire. Suffering from a broken marriage, I gather, and hasn't quite got over it.' He paused significantly. 'If you see what I mean.'

It seemed they all did. Their unified sigh of sympathy and understanding for a deeply disturbed patient only just disguised Kate's gasp of outrage.

'We had to take her in,' Richard continued. 'To leave her there by herself—well, I certainly couldn't have answered for the consequences.' He spread his hands helplessly. 'I know I've broken every rule in the book, but what would you have me do?'

There were sympathetic nods and murmurs. Kate shook her head in stunned amazement. It seemed that Richard Blair would once more get his own way.

'Could I let Matron show you Theatre and the kitchens?' Richard asked politely. He gestured back to Kate's room and Kate's slightly opened door closed swiftly. 'Your visit may have distressed my patient—I need to check.'

'Of course, Dr Blair.' They were putty in his hand. 'It seems the town's doubly fortunate you were available to take patients,' they told him.

Two minutes later Richard walked into Kate's room again, this time alone. In his hand he bore a small suitcase.

Kate was sitting on the edge of the bed, her eyes smouldering. She was silent as he walked in and laid the case on the bed.

'How's my favourite patient this morning?' he grinned. 'Distressed by so many visitors?'

'I'm not suicidal, if that's what you mean,' Kate said grimly. 'More like homicidal.'

'I knew I was right to admit you,' Richard smiled. 'There's no telling what you would have done if I'd left you to suffer at home.'

'Only if you were within throwing distance. Richard Blair, how dared you insinuate I was unbalanced?'

'He who dares, wins,' Richard said lightly. 'Do you think a sprained ankle is a good reason for being in an unlicensed hospital?'

'No, I do not, and well you know it.'

'Well, that's very fortunate, because I'm about to discharge you,' Richard said briskly. He unzipped the suitcase. 'They've been told we have two efficient doctors in town, so two efficient doctors they must see. Pete's taxi is outside waiting. Can you be dressed and down at the surgery in half an hour?'

'Half an hour?' Kate squeaked.

'I know, I know.' He spread his hands helplessly. 'It takes you longer than that to apply your false eyelashes. But this is an emergency. Kate, I'm depending on you.'

'Depending on a morbidly depressed, lovesick and suicidal patient who wanders around freezing houses naked! You must be kidding, Dr Blair.'

He grinned. 'I'm a miracle worker, Dr Harris. I've just pronounced you cured.' He eyed the crutches in the corner of the room. 'Use those to get to the car but try not to let the team see them.'

'Just in case they might not be as silly as you hope they are,' Kate said waspishly. She grabbed the case. 'I make no promises. . .' She stopped short. 'These aren't my clothes.'

Richard had walked to the door. 'Well, no,' he said apologetically. 'I was damned if I'd let my partner be seen in that drab grey skirt.' He looked ruefully down at his dark suit. 'If I can look the part so can you. Consider this your uniform, Dr Harris.'

Kate lifted a soft pale blue dress from the case. It was of fine lambswool, beautifully cut and just her size. 'H-how did you. . .?' She was stuttering.

'With a bit of help from Bella Quayle. Oh, and Nan from Nan's Frocks. She was delighted to open on

Sunday afternoon for such a worthy cause.' He grinned.
'See you in half an hour.'

Kate was left staring in stunned silence at the closed
door.

It took her minutes to get her breath back. Finally
she found the strength to examine the contents of the
case.

The case held more than the dress. There was
beautiful, quality lingerie, opaque tights in soft grey to
complement the dress and grey-blue shoes to match.
Everything was just Kate's size and she realised her
own clothes had been used to gauge her fitting.

Her face burned with mortification. Her own clothes
weren't that bad. Or were they? Her fingers clenched
and reclenched as she thought of her appearance since
Doug had left. She had taken no trouble at all. Her
skirt and blouses had been serviceable, dull and dowdy,
and she hadn't cared. She put the soft lambswool of the
pretty dress up to her cheek and a feeling of pleasure
she had almost forgotten ran through her. Good-quality
clothes. . .

But to wear clothes bought by that man. . . How
could she?

It was that or appear in the surgery wearing a hospital
gown. To her horror Kate heard voices coming back
along the corridor. She glanced at her watch. Five
minutes of Richard's stipulated time had slipped away
already.

At least he hasn't bought me false eyelashes, she
smiled reluctantly to herself. Move, Katy Harris.

She moved.

Ten minutes later she was surveying herself thoughtfully in the mirror. A Kate Harris she had almost
forgotten existed stared back at her. The soft blue dress
clung to her slim figure, accentuating the shapeliness of
her form. It had long sleeves and a shawl collar, but the
clinging wool disguised nothing. Her firm, taut breasts

stood out, startling her. For the last two years she had
disguised her sexuality. This dress — well, it certainly
didn't disguise it, she thought ruefully.

'There had better be a white coat at the surgery,' she
muttered to herself, carefully removing her bandage.
The tights were thick and supporting, and would help
to brace her injured ankle, at least until she had been
assessed. She placed her new shoes on with trepidation,
but they were made of soft leather and were cut low.
They didn't hurt.

To her disgust there was make-up in the case. She
rejected it with a glance and then thought better of it,
applying a soft powder to her cheeks to try and subdue
the burning colour. Finally she brushed her hair until it
shone a burnished gold. She would have liked to tie it
back, but there was no ribbon or pins. It was destined
to be loose. Finally she caught her crutches and hopped
to the door.

There were still voices in the corridor outside.

'We didn't do a comprehensive inspection of Room
Two,' a voice was saying. Kate winced. Room Two was
hers.

'I'm afraid I'll have to ask that my patient isn't further
disturbed,' Richard said quietly. 'She really is quite
unstable. . .'

'You're telling me,' Kate whispered grimly, holding
on to her crutches and wobbling. They were harder to
use than she thought. And how was she going to get to
the car park if the team were still in the corridor? Wait
till they left? They'd reach the surgery before she did.
Finally she crossed to the window and soundlessly lifted
it. 'I'm as mad as he is,' she muttered. Carefully she
lowered her crutches out on to the garden and climbed
out after them.

The garden was hard to negotiate with the crutches.
The tips kept sinking into the moist winter ground and
a couple of times she stumbled. She made it halfway to

the car park before Pete, the taxi driver, came running through the trees towards her.

'Good on you, Doc,' he said triumphantly. 'I knew you'd make it.' Then, as he drew nearer, he stopped short, staring in amazement. 'Geepers, Doc. What have you done to yourself?'

'I've sprained my ankle,' Kate said shortly, concentrating on keeping the crutches upright.

Pete shook his head. 'It's not your ankle I'm talking about,' he told her. 'Wow!' He took her arm and supported her on. 'We're doing well,' he said encouragingly. 'We've still ten minutes.'

'Do you know what Dr Blair is doing?' Kate managed. She was having trouble keeping her breath.

'Reckon the whole town does,' Pete grinned. 'We'll get this bloody hospital accredited or bust!'

Kate shook her head in wonder, and then concentrated hard on keeping her footing.

Five minutes later Pete's battered taxi drew up in front of the surgery beside Alf's pharmacy. Kate stared at the little building she had eyed so wistfully for so long. A new brass plate swung proudly on the door.

'Dr Richard Blair', it proclaimed, 'MB.ChB. FRCGP', and 'Dr Kate Harris, MB.BS.Dip.Obs.'

The sign said she belonged. The sign said she was where she wanted to be.

She shook her head in disbelief. This was not the way she had envisaged starting work in this surgery. Still, just now was no time for reflection. Pete was already out of the taxi, holding the crutches and waiting for her to alight.

'OK, Dr Harris, MB.BS. Dip.Obs,' Kate muttered to herself. 'Let's start work.'

CHAPTER NINE

BELLA was already ensconced behind the gleaming new receptionist desk. She rose swiftly as Kate entered and came forward to take Pete's place beside her.

'Welcome to work, Dr Harris.' Bella was obviously suffering from nerves. She glanced at her watch. 'There's still a couple of moments to go. Mrs Larkin is in your room with little David. His card is on your desk.'

It was all Kate could do not to gasp in amazement. She had been in this building before, a barren little shell, stripped bare of its fitting. Now it was a vibrant, warm little surgery, with a waiting-room packed with patients. The furnishings were tasteful and carefully chosen. Every detail had been carefully considered, right down to the chalk board hanging low on one wall where two small children were engaged in the execution of a major work of art.

Apart from the two small artists every eye in the waiting-room was on Kate.

'You're doing us proud, Doc Harris,' an old man from the corner told her. Kate recognised Sam, Bert King's brother. 'You'll get this thing done.'

'Are you really all patients or are you just here for show?' Kate asked slowly, and there was a general laugh.

'Reckon we're real enough,' Sam King told her. 'But Bella here tells us we'll be in for a bit of a wait. She's packed us in like to show them city blokes we really need the service Doc Blair's setting up.'

Kate shook her head. Then, at the sound of vehicles pulling up outside, Bella tugged her through to the inner sanctum with 'Dr Harris' on the door. Mrs Larkin was waiting.

'I need a white coat,' Kate whispered desperately. She looked down at her dress. 'I can't meet them like this.'

Bella grabbed a white coat from behind Kate's door and swiftly helped Kate into it. Kate reached for the buttons and stopped.

'Where are the buttons?' she asked suspiciously.

'We took 'em off,' Bella confessed. 'Nan and I decided it'd look better this way. Efficient but we can still see your lovely dress.'

'But I want buttons,' Kate hissed.

Bella was propelling her urgently to the chair behind the desk. 'I haven't time to sew them on now,' she said. 'See you later.' She walked swiftly out, closing the door. Kate was left smiling weakly at Mrs Larkin.

Rather to her surprise. Mrs Larkin's problem was real. David had a nasty ear infection. The child's temperature was up and he was miserable and listless. Despite the sounds coming from the waiting-room, Kate was able to concentrate on the problem at hand, reassuring the listless child huddled on his mother's lap.

'The antibiotics should start having an effect within twelve hours,' she told them. 'And meanwhile we'll give you something for the pain.' She smiled reassuringly at the little boy and bent her head to write a script.

There was a tentative knock on the door.

'Yes?' Kate called, in what she hoped was an efficient tone. Bella's head appeared around the door.

'Dr Blair and the people from the Health Commission are here,' Bella told her. 'They'd like to meet you. Can I bring them in when Mrs Larkin leaves?'

'Yes,' Kate said in a harried tone, knowing that her

voice was carrying to the outside room. 'How far behind am I?'

'About forty minutes,' Bella said apologetically. 'And Dr Blair doesn't think he'll be in until this afternoon.'

Kate sighed. 'Very well.' Bella closed the door and she and the Larkins were left alone.

Two minutes later she ushered Mrs Larkin back out into the reception area. The waiting-room was packed, with patients and team members. To her relief Kate realised it would be silly for her to emerge to talk to them. The quietest place was in her room. She stepped back inside, innocuously — she hoped — holding the edge of the desk. Her crutches had been whisked away by Bella.

'Dr Harris.' The chairman came in first and held out his hand. 'Pleased to meet you.' He turned to introduce the other four team members filing in.

'I'm sorry about the crowd,' Kate smiled, shaking each hand in turn. She was standing beside her desk, leaning very carefully against its supporting weight. 'I would have liked to be down at the hospital to meet you but. . .' She spread her hands expressively. 'I'm sorry.'

'Don't apologise, Dr Harris,' the chairman beamed. He was obviously becoming more and more impressed with this efficient little medical service. 'We're just amazed you've managed without a hospital for so long.'

Kate shrugged. 'Without another doctor there was no way I could reopen the hospital,' she said simply. 'And finding another doctor with the desire to come here was almost impossible. The current belief among medical trainees is that you'd have to be crazy to take up country practice.' She couldn't prevent a slightly malicious smile across at Richard as she said the word crazy. He smiled right back.

'I think that describes the pair of us,' he said cheerfully. 'Crazy.'

'Perhaps you are,' the chairman smiled. 'To sink so much into an investment as tenuous as a small bush nursing hospital. . .' He turned to the other team members. 'I think we agree, do we not, ladies and gentlemen, that it requires a huge degree of courage and faith?' At their nods of agreement he turned back.

'We'll not hold you up any longer, Dr Harris,' he told her. 'Any further technicalities can be ironed out with Dr Blair. But we do congratulate the pair of you on a fine little service. It won't be us who'll be throwing impediments in your way.'

Kate smiled limply. The strain of standing on her ankle was beginning to tell.

'Thanks, Kate,' Richard smiled. 'I'll be back to help as soon as possible.' He gestured to the waiting-room. 'It's nice to be needed.'

One of the team members had paused at the door, a thought occurring to her.

'Dr Harris, this may sound insulting, but I would like to know before we leave just how committed you are to the valley. Dr Blair, it seems, has sunk a lot of his own money into the medical service. You, however. . .' She let the question trail off. 'Are you likely to leave in the near future? It seems a little risky to set up a hospital when there's a chance Dr Blair will be left alone.'

Kate cast a swift look at Richard. For once he left the talking to her. Should she admit she was leaving three weeks from now? Richard's precious hospital would be jeopardised if she did so.

'It's hardly me you need to worry about,' Kate said slowly. 'I've been in the valley for two years. Dr Blair on the other hand seems much more volatile.'

The committee members smiled as though she had just made a joke. 'He's hardly likely to leave after

investing as much as he has,' the woman said. 'You, on
the other hand. . . Have you invested in this project as
well?'

'I don't think you need to worry about Dr Harris's
commitment,' Richard said, smiling possessively across
at Kate. He crossed to give her a quick hug, taking the
pressure off her injured ankle for a blessed moment.
'Dr Harris and I are partners in more than one sense of
the word.'

'Oh. . .' The woman interrogating them looked from
Kate's flaming cheeks to Richard's smiling face. 'Oh, I
see.' She smiled broadly. 'Well, isn't that nice? How
fortunate for the community.'

'Not just for the community,' Richard said, tighten-
ing his hold on Kate.

Kate's colour deepened. Any minute now I'll snap,
she thought desperately.

'I think that's all we need to know,' the chairman
said pleasantly. 'We'll leave you to get back to your
patients, Dr Harris.'

The other members of the team filed out. The
woman, however, paused again at the door as Richard
attempted to usher her out.

'You have such unusual hair, Dr Harris. The lass in
the hospital has just such a shade of chestnut. It's
strange to see it twice in one day.'

Kate drew in her breath, desperately seeking for a
response, but Richard was before her.

'It's a shade you'll see often in the valley,' he told the
woman. 'This place his been isolated for generations.
Even now it's a forty-minute car trip to the next town
worthy of the name. The genetic pool has been pretty
limited.' He paused thoughtfully. 'I often wonder
whether that's the underlying cause of problems such
as you saw in our young patient.'

Kate gasped. She turned to Richard, her eyes flashing. The woman, on the other hand, smiled in understanding.

'It's just as well you're an outsider, then,' she told Richard. 'It will be nice for the valley to have some fresh blood. . .' And she walked out.

Kate was left smouldering at Richard. His arm was still around her waist.

'I don't believe what you just said,' she gasped. 'Even if I did come from the valley. . .'

'Which you don't,' he nodded, bending to kiss her firmly on the lips. 'I know. The inbreeding wouldn't account for the lunatic element. There has to be a deeper cause.' He sighed dolefully and kissed her again. 'It's up to me to keep searching.'

'Take your hands off me. . .'

He held his hands up in mock-surrender. 'OK, Dr Harris. You win.' He crossed to the door which the woman had closed behind her. 'I'd better take our inspection panel down to the hotel for morning coffee and a bout of form-filling. Will you be OK here?'

'How many of those patients outside are real and how many have been planted for the occasion?' Kate asked suspiciously.

'They're all above-board,' Richard said, in an offended tone. 'I'm doing nothing dishonest.'

'No.' Kate hopped back to her desk and lowered herself gingerly back into her chair. 'I just hope for your sake they don't demand another quick check of the hospital, with Room Two included.'

'There'd be nothing wrong with that,' Richard smiled. 'Our erratic young lady discharged herself this morning. Really, I am concerned about her. I left Matron ringing the local constabulary. It seems she was so distraught she even left through the bedroom window. . .' He shook his head. 'It's all the same with the redheads in this valley. I think we might have to consider a psychiatric wing. . .'

He walked out and gently closed the door behind him. Kate was left staring open-mouthed, not knowing whether to laugh or cry.

She had time for neither. Richard had not been kidding when he'd said most of the patients in the waiting-room were there for genuine problems, although Kate suspected many of the problems had been brought along for airing to check out the new surgery. And the new doctor, of course, although most of them were too polite to voice disappointment when Richard took his time returning.

Kate worked on. Richard must be lunching them in style, she thought ruefully, checking her wrist-watch after one. More money. . .

There was little she could do about it. Most of the patients she was seeing were known to her. They were all expressing pleasure as seeing her as part of the new medical service.

'And Dr Blair's lovely, isn't he?' old Mrs Featherstone smiled at her. 'Really, dear, I couldn't be more pleased if you were my own daughter.'

Kate flushed. She looked up from examining the fading rash from the old lady's shingles and met the twinkling eyes.

'You can get any thoughts like that right out of your head,' she said severely. 'Honestly, Mrs Featherstone, I've been married and I'm past that nonsense.'

'You're never too old,' the gnarled and wrinkled lady told her. 'I was Mrs Bennett until I was sixty-seven and five years after Mr Bennet died I became Mrs Featherstone. And if Archie Featherstone and I aren't past it, I don't see how you can be.'

Kate shook her head at the old lady, smiling in spite of herself. 'How are you getting on with the itch?' she asked. The rash extended down the elderly lady's back and under her right arm.

'I'm getting better,' Mrs Featherstone told her.

'Though what I would have done if I didn't have Archie to rub my ointment in I don't know. Though it is exhausting. . .'

'Exhausting?'

'I never yet knew a man who could give you a massage without wanting something else,' the old lady twinkled. She shook her head at Kate. 'Too old, my eye. I don't know what the world's coming to.'

Kate smiled and lifted the next card from the pile before her. Mrs Westruther and daughter. . .

Mrs Westruther was destined to wait. The sound of raised voices in the waiting-room made Kate lift her head. Edna Featherstone was struggling into the first of several layers of clothes. Leaving her to it, Kate hobbled painfully out into the reception area.

It was Alf, the pharmacist from next door. Kate sighed inwardly. Now what? Alf Burrows had done nothing but make trouble for Kate since she had come to the valley. His personal vendetta against women doctors amounted almost to an obsession.

'You can't do this,' Bella was saying weakly.

'I already have done it,' the elderly pharmacist cackled. 'And you needn't tell me I can't, Bella Quayle, because it's my pharmacy and I'll fill out the prescriptions I please. And now we've a proper doctor in the town I don't see any need to take orders from any woman calling herself a doctor. . .'

Kate took a deep breath. 'Good afternoon, Mr Burrows.'

Alf turned to face her. His face wrinkled into a grin. 'Good afternoon, miss,' he said politely.

'What seems to be the trouble?' Kate said quietly.

The pharmacist shrugged. 'If I'd known Doc Blair was thinking of letting you into the place when I sold him this surgery I'd have had second thoughts,' he told her. 'I've been on to my lawyer this morning and it seems I don't have any come-back. But I'm damned if I'll continue to take orders from any woman. . .'

'Filling prescriptions is hardly taking orders,' Kate told him.

'It seems so to me, miss.' Alf met her look with a belligerent stare. 'And I'm responsible for these folks' health. I've been a pharmacist here for nigh on thirty years, and I'm darned if I'll dispense medicine ordered by a woman calling herself a doctor any longer.' He shrugged. 'When there was no other doctor here it seemed I had no choice. But these people have a fine doctor now in Doc Blair and they should know it. So I'll be filling no more of your prescriptions, miss,' he said firmly. 'Unless they're countersigned by Doc Blair, of course. I don't mind if he's checked them.'

'But I can't work under those conditions,' Kate said slowly. 'And if I don't work the hospital can't go ahead.'

'Sure it can,' Alf retorted. 'All I'm saying is that you've got to get your work countersigned by a competent doctor.'

'And I'm not?'

'You're a woman,' Alf said disparagingly. 'I'm sure you do your best and you filled in OK when there wasn't a doctor in town — like the women in war work when their men were away — but it's time you stood aside now and let Doc Blair take over.'

Around the small waiting-room the waiting patients watched in silence. The room was filled with a deathly hush. Kate closed her eyes, willing her temper to stay down. Then, in the hush, Richard's voice sounded.

'What do you mean, you won't fill my partner's scripts?'

Unnoticed, Richard had appeared at the outer door. He stood, watchful, taking in the tableau in front of him. Alf wheeled to face him, smiling ingratiatingly.

'Dr Blair. Welcome aboard. Ready to take over here,

I hope? I've just been explaining the new rules to your assistant here.' His voice emphasised the word *assistant*.

'Dr Harris is not my assistant,' Richard said harshly. 'Dr Harris is my partner. And I'll thank you to treat her accordingly. What's more, as she's been here for two years and I start work today, she's officially senior partner. If you have any problems with filling her prescriptions I suggest you take it up with the pharmaceutical board, because that's who we'll be taking it up with if one — just one — of our prescriptions is refused.'

'You never told me *she* was coming to work here,' the old man spat. 'You bought this place under false pretences. If I'd known you were bringing in a woman——'

'It's you who told the lies,' Richard said icily. 'You failed to tell me Dr Harris was already practising as Corrook's doctor when I bought the surgery.' Richard's brown eyes were hard as steel. 'In fact, you deliberately told me there was no doctor within forty miles. In a court of law I could have you up for misrepresentation.'

'If you want to declare the sale void I'm sure I could accommodate you,' Alf hissed. 'I won't work with a woman doctor.'

'You haven't a choice,' Richard said grimly. Turning his back on the pharmacist, he took a card from Bella's lifeless hand. 'Is this for me, Mrs Quayle?'

'N-no,' Bella stammered. 'This one's for Dr Harris. I've kept those wanting to see you separate.'

'I'm not filling her scripts and that's final,' Alf said to Richard's back. He turned to Kate. 'So you might as well pack your bags and take yourself off.'

'You fail to fill script for Dr Harris and I'll have you before the pharmaceutical board faster than you can blink,' Richard said evenly, without turning.

'Yeah?' The elderly pharmacist dug his hands into the pockets of his shabby tweed coat. 'You know how long those cases take to come up?' He chuckled. 'I'll be due for retirement by the time you have me struck off, even if you do. To be honest, I've been wanting to retire for a while. Sticking the spoke into this new-fangled feminist medicine seems as good a way as any to go out.'

Kate shook her head in amazement. She knew the pharmacist resented her, but she hadn't known the dislike was so intense.

'Alf, this is silly,' she said softly. 'You've been filling my prescriptions for two years now.'

'Only because I had no choice, miss,' Alf snapped. 'Anyway, I've said my piece.' He walked to the door.

'Just a moment.' Richard's authoritative tone stopped him in his tracks. Alf turned to look.

Richard was holding the pile of patient cards in his hand, frowning down at them. There was a long silence. Around the room the patients were also quiet. Even the children drawing at the chalk board sensed the tension and turned to look.

'Is that your final word?' Richard asked. His voice was quiet, and suddenly menacing.

'It is,' Alf said. 'Take it or leave it, young man.'

'You'll fill prescriptions signed by me but not my partner?'

'That's right.'

Kate shook her head helplessly. This was crazy. 'Richard, I'm going to leave anyway——' she began.

'Keep out of this, Dr Harris,' Richard snapped. He placed the patient cards on the table.

'I won't be writing any prescriptions, then,' Richard said slowly. 'Not one. All my prescriptions will be sighted and signed only by Dr Harris. I'll not have you destroy this partnership with your blind prejudice.'

'You can't do that,' Alf sneered. 'You can't practise if you can't write prescriptions.'

'As it happens, Dr Harris is deskbound for the next couple of weeks,' Richard told him. His tone was indifferent. 'It will be a minor inconvenience for patients to have their prescriptions made out by Dr Harris after I've seen them, but I'm sure the town will be understanding. And if the only prescriptions available are those of Dr Harris, once more you won't have a choice. The population of the valley will very soon have something to say if they have to travel forty miles to have a prescription filled.'

'You can't keep that up forever,' Alf snarled.

'I have no intention of doing so.' Richard was at his most urbane. 'You're correct in that it will be an inconvenience. However, I don't anticipate having to do it for very long.'

Because she was leaving, Kate thought bleakly. Had Richard accepted it, then?

Richard picked up his top card. 'Mr Burt?' he said enquiringly, looking round the waiting-room. A small, wiry man stood up and took off his hat.

'Here, Doc.'

'Come through, please,' Richard smiled. 'Oh, and Mr Burt?'

'Yeah?'

'If you need a prescription, will you mind waiting a moment after your appointment while Mrs Quayle takes it through to be signed by Dr Harris?'

The little man looked over at Alf and grinned. 'It'd be a pleasure to do so,' he told Richard firmly. 'Kate Harris has been a darned fine GP in this valley for the last two years. If you'll support her now, you'll find the valley is right behind you.'

Richard smiled. 'Thank you, Mr Burt.' He glanced across at Kate. 'Is there anything else, Dr Harris?'

'I don't. . . I don't think so,' Kate said weakly. Alf was standing by the door, his mouth agape. Kate tried hard not to look at him.

'Then I suggest you see your next patient,' Richard said kindly.

CHAPTER TEN

KATE worked solidly for the rest of the afternoon, scarcely drawing breath between patients. The signing of Richard's prescriptions took time, and it added to a surgery where patients were more curious than ill. As such they took longer than usual. A patient with an earache was relatively easy to cope with. It took longer to cope with patients with niggling worries which had surfaced only because there was so much going on in the new doctors' surgery. Mostly those worries were so trivial they could have remained safely unaired for another twelve months, but occasionally an airing paid off.

'It's this darned mole on my back, Doc,' the local grocer told Kate. 'I knocked it a while back and it won't heal. It keeps bleeding and it seems to be getting bigger if anything.'

With a sinking heart Kate recognised it for what it was. She couldn't be a hundred per cent sure, but it had the classic signs of a melanoma.

'I'm not going to the city to get it cut off,' Ron Clarke told her, horrified, when she outlined what she thought should happen. 'That thing? It's only an infected knock.'

'If I was sure it was harmless I wouldn't be sending you to the city,' Kate said gently. 'But it may be a melanoma, and if it is you're going to have to have it excised carefully. The area around it will have to be removed as well, and that's going to require a skin graft by a plastic surgeon.' She met the man's eyes directly, seeing the seed of fear there. She couldn't avoid it. It was better to be honest. If she was mistaken — and she

126

hoped she was — Ron would be only too happy to hear her mistake. 'I could test it here, but if it is a melanoma then I've disturbed it, and possibly caused spread. I'd like you to go where they can do the pathology on the spot.'

Ron sat back in his chair and looked at her. 'And then what?'

Kate smiled reassuringly. 'Ron, if it is a melanoma, then we've caught it early. There's a very good chance it will cause you no more trouble.'

'But it might.'

'There is a chance,' Kate said honestly.

The man laughed shortly. 'Is this my surfing youth coming back to haunt me?'

'Probably,' Kate admitted. 'Did you do much?'

'All the time. I spent every spare moment of every summer on my board. And I used to reckon I tanned easily too. I scoffed at kids who wore shirts or sun cream.'

Kate sighed. 'I'm sorry, Ron,' she said. 'But at least you came early. And it may well prove to be nothing.'

'Yeah, well, that's my luck.' Ron attempted a smile. 'To tell you the truth I was just looking for an excuse to check this place out, though the wife's been at me for a week or so to get this seen. Seemed a good excuse.'

Kate wrote a referral and handed it over. 'Have Bella ring before you leave the surgery,' she told him. 'I want you seen this week.'

'Sure thing.' He stood up and twisted his hands. 'If it spreads, Doc, what then?'

Kate stood as well. She limped round and put a hand on his arm. 'Let's cross that bridge when we come to it,' she said firmly. 'We don't even know whether the thing's malignant or not.'

'You mean you really don't know?'

'I don't know it's melanoma, and I have no way of

knowing if it will spread if it is,' Kate said firmly. 'If I did, I'd tell you, Ron. You can trust me on that.'

He looked at her for a long moment. 'I do,' he said at last. 'Thanks, Kate.'

Ron left and Bella came in bearing a couple more scripts. Kate sighed. Richard's scripts had to be rewritten as well as just signed. She had worked out very quickly that just to sign his scripts would not be enough. Alf could tell who had written them.

Finally the last patient was seen and Kate bade him goodbye with relief. She sat at her desk filling in her day sheets until Richard knocked and entered. She looked up and then kept on writing. Soundlessly he came around and looked over her shoulder at what she was writing.

'Tired?'

'Mmm.' She was acutely aware of his presence and her fingers slowed in their writing.

'I'll have to pay you more if you keep on at this rate,' he said softly. His large hands dropped on to her shoulders and started massaging the tired muscles.

'They. . . It won't always be this busy.' Kate's body was doing strange things. The pen didn't seem to want to work at all. 'It's only because you're new.'

'I know that. I'll clear out of the surgery tomorrow and let you do it on your own. At least then you won't be wasting time rewriting my scripts, and if I'm not here the curious might stay away.'

Kate forced her pen to keep moving. Richard's hands continued their gentle rubbing. She could feel her tension dissipating through their strength.

'You don't have to do that,' she managed to say.

'If it were a duty I wouldn't be,' Richard told her firmly. 'I'm enjoying myself.'

'And I'm trying to work.'

'You've finished.' He took the last patient's card and

compared it to the day sheet. All done. 'Were your patients all tyre kickers?'

'Tyre kickers?'

'Checking out the new surgery?'

Kate smiled and rose awkwardly to her feet. Richard's hands held her. He was so darned close. His masculinity enveloped her, and even her good ankle seemed weak.

'Not. . .not all.' She made an effort to regain her professional calm and told him of Ron's melanoma.

'Are you sure it is?' Richard asked.

'Not a hundred per cent,' Kate admitted. 'But sure enough not to risk doing the excision here.'

'It'd be better if we had our own pathology lab,' Richard said slowly.

Kate shook her head. 'It's too big,' she told him. 'It's going to need a skin graft.'

'OK. But things that don't. . .' Richard frowned. 'I'll look into it.'

'Don't you think it'd be better to recoup some of the money you've ploughed into the place before putting more money in?' Kate said harshly. 'Honestly. . .'

Richard shook his head and smiled, refusing to be drawn. 'You've no vision, Kate,' he told her sadly.

Kate drew in her breath. She had heard that line so many times before. Doug had used it over and over, seemingly every time she enquired into any of his business dealings.

'Now what did I say to make you recoil?' Richard demanded. The laugh had died from his eyes and he was staring intently down at her.

'Nothing.' Kate pulled away from the hands resting lightly on her waist. 'If you'll excuse me, Dr Blair, I need to go home.'

'To your cold house and empty cupboards?' he asked sardonically.

Kate stared at him blankly and he sighed.

'Honestly, Katy Harris, what did you do before I chanced on the scene? Starve?'

'I did very nicely,' Kate snapped. 'At least I didn't have to spend half my working day rewriting someone else's prescriptions.'

'That's a bit unfair.'

Kate bit her lip and flushed, forced to accept the justice of his accusation. 'I know,' she admitted. 'I'm sorry.' She kept her head down, avoiding his gaze. 'Richard, that can't go on, though. How long do you propose not being able to write a script?'

'I'll write the urgent ones,' Richard said. 'If I have to I will. But all the routine stuff can be rewritten until—'

'Until when?' Kate shook her head. 'Alf's as stubborn as a mule. He's been losing money hand over fist for two years by not leasing me this surgery but he wouldn't give in. Do you think he'll back down?'

'No,' Richard said. 'But the man's nearing seventy. It's time he retired.'

'So you'll take him to the pharmaceutical board.'

'No.' Richard lifted the white coat from her shoulders and hung it on the hook on the back of the door. 'I have other plans, which may or may not come to fruition. Meanwhile, I'll keep sending my scripts to you. May I tell you how much I approve of your outfit, Dr Harris?' His eyes were warm with admiration and the laughter was back.

Kate's colour mounted. His eyes were a caress.

'As you gave me no choice, you can hardly compliment my taste in clothing,' she said bitterly. 'Nan and Bella enjoyed themselves, no doubt.'

'Not just Nan and Bella,' Richard told her in an aggrieved tone. 'I helped.'

'I prefer to choose my own clothes.' She grabbed her crutches from behind her desk and hopped towards the door.

'As soon as we find a locum we'll take a trip to the city together and you can do just that,' Richard promised. 'Nan's selection is rather limited.'

Kate wheeled around to face him. 'Richard Blair, will you leave me alone?' she flung at him. 'If you think I'll stand meekly by while you take over my life, while you steal my practice, fling me in hospital, dress me as you want. . .' She choked on her anger. Shoving past, she made for the door. The mat at the entrance caught the tip of her crutch. She stumbled but Richard was beside her, steadying her.

'Someone has to,' he said mildly. 'It doesn't seem to me that you're doing all that efficient a job of running your life alone.'

Kate wrenched her hand from his. She limped to the phone.

'What are you doing?' Richard enquired.

'Ringing for a taxi.'

'I'll take you home.'

'Over my dead body,' she snapped.

'That's a bit extreme.' And then, as her anger caught on a tiny choke of involuntary laughter, he moved to replace the receiver on the cradle. 'That's better, my Kate.' He touched her nose lightly with his finger. 'Now, if you'll control that temper for a moment, we have an admission to do. Bert King arrived back by ambulance this afternoon and I thought we'd see him together.'

Kate's eyes lit up. 'Bert. . . Oh, how is he?'

Richard shook his head. 'Your guess is as good as mine. I haven't seen him yet. He's your patient.'

Kate hesitated. 'You have to go to the hospital anyway?'

'I have to check on Sophie. So if you ring for a taxi, your taxi will be following my car.' He smiled. 'Crazy, isn't it?'

It was. If there was one thing Richard Blair seemed

good at it was getting his own way. Kate gave an inward shrug. She was getting more dependent on the man every moment.

'Fine,' she said ungraciously. 'Pinch my patients. Push me into hospital. Dress me as you please. Take me where you want. I'll be a nice pliable partner for the next three weeks. But you'd better be looking fast for another partner to take over then, Richard Blair. Because as soon as my three weeks is over I'm off. Regardless of what I let the Health Commission team think. After three weeks is up, my life is my own again.'

'Three weeks is a very long time,' Richard said thoughtfully.

'You're telling me,' Kate snapped.

Bert King was sitting up in bed waiting for them. He grinned as the two doctors approached and stared with interest at Kate's crutches.

'I'm supposed to be the one with the sore legs,' he complained. 'I'm getting pipped at the post all over the place.'

'You mean Sophie?' Kate smiled. She didn't have to examine Bert to tell that he was better. The twinkle was firmly back in the old man's eyes. It had been driven out by constant pain, and Kate was delighted to greet its return. She took the old man's hand in hers and grinned mischievously. 'I knew Dr Blair couldn't be trusted,' she confided to Bert. 'Making rash promises like you being the first patient here. If I were you I'd sue him for thousands.'

The old man's toothless mouth wrinkled into another grin. 'I would,' he said firmly. 'But Sophie's my brother's grandkid. And Sam'd never forgive me.'

'You've seen Sam already, then?' Kate asked.

'Sure have.' The old man practically bounced on his bed. 'I got back at four, and since then I've had five visitors.' He held up his hand. 'Sam. Sophie's mum and dad. Bella Quayle.' He wrinkled his nose. 'Oh, and the parson.'

'Probably the parson's the one you need most,' Richard said severely from the door.

'Yeah, well, I was thinking that before I went away,' Bert admitted. 'But me legs are healing so well I reckon there's time and to spare to repent.'

'Repent what?' Kate asked mischievously.

'Never you mind, miss,' Bert told her. He winked up at Richard. 'Women,' he sighed. 'They'll ask a man anything.'

Kate had perched on the edge of the bed and was carefully unwrapping Bert's legs. What she saw there made her let out her breath in an exclamation of pleasure.

'Oh, Bert, these are excellent!'

'I know,' Bert said smugly. 'I got down to that city hospital and thought, Well, if I've got to be here, I'm damned if I don't make the most out of it. So I had physiotherapy and occupational therapy and every other damned therapy till it was coming out my ears. And I ate everything they put in front of me — even when it was something called lassarna which was so damned slimy it slid down without me even having to put me teeth in. . .'

'Lasagne?' Kate smiled.

'Yeah. Lassarna. And I'll say something for you, young fella.' He pointed a bony finger at Richard. 'You've done one sensible thing. You've employed the best damned cook in the valley in Mrs Fry. She's just been round and promised me roast beef and three veggies for me dinner. None of this new-fangled lassarna muck about Mrs Fry.' He indicated the glass beside the bed in which his dentures lay in state. 'She'll cook me something worth putting me teeth in for.'

The doctors left him contemplating his dinner with supreme satisfaction. Kate couldn't contain her glow of pleasure. She had been worried about Bert for months. If he kept improving at his present rate he'd be home in a week, fitter than he had been for years.

'Thank you, Richard,' she said impulsively as they walked out of the door.

Richard raised his eyebrows. 'I don't believe what I'm hearing.'

Kate smiled ruefully. 'I know I'm critical,' she said. 'But you are doing a few good things. I guess if the hospital folds tomorrow at least Sophie's alive and Bert looks like having a few more good years at home.'

'The hospital won't fold.'

Kate shrugged. She had said what she wanted to say.

They checked Sophie, who was improving hourly and wanting to know when the irritating drip could be removed from the vein in her hand.

'Not for another day or so,' Richard told her sternly. 'I'm not risking a really fancy piece of sewing with infection.'

Sophie giggled. 'Is it really a fancy piece of sewing?' she asked.

'You bet.' Richard checked the little girl's obs and smiled down at her. 'I'm thinking of taking up patchwork.'

Sophie smiled back up. 'You know, I don't even mind about short hair?' she confided.

'I'm pleased about that.'

'Dr Blair?'

'Yes?'

Sophie looked uncertainly from Kate to Richard and then back again. 'Dr Blair, are you going to marry Dr Harris?'

'Sophie!' Kate flushed deep red and bit her lip. 'Sophie Mannaway, there are some questions you just don't ask.'

'That's what Mum said,' Sophie sighed. 'But how else do you find out if you don't ask?'

'Very true,' Richard told her. He grinned across at Kate. 'Well, Dr Harris?'

'I've had one husband, Sophie,' Kate told the little girl. 'And I'm not in the market for another.' She bit her lip, striving to keep her voice light. 'And even if I were, I think I could find one less bossy than Dr Blair, don't you think?'

Sophie snuggled down on her pillows. 'I don't think he's bossy,' she said sleepily. 'I think he's nice.'

'And what further recommendation can you require?' Richard demanded.

Kate made no demur when Richard ushered her into his car. She was feeling slightly dazed, as though she was only half awake. Too much had happened too fast. Life was spinning past out of control. She sat silently as Richard shrugged off his suit coat and pulled on his beloved sweater. 'That's better,' he grinned.

As they edged out of the hospital car park he smiled across at her sympathetically.

'You've worked too hard today, lass,' he said gently. 'Given an easier boss you should have had another couple of days off.'

'My foot's hardly hurting,' Kate said truthfully. The feeling of unreality was deepening. Richard's sympathy was worse than his overbearing ways. When he ruled her life she could be angry. When he looked at her with those eyes that were both compassionate and caring she felt reality slip further and further away.

'Let's hope for a quiet night, then.' Richard turned the car radio on to something soft and soothing.

'I don't see why you should have the night off,' Kate managed. 'Today was your first day back at work.'

'As if I haven't been working like a navvy for the past month,' Richard said. 'Ever since I saw this place. . .'

They fell silent, both deep in their own thoughts. Kate risked a glance across at the man beside her. His

eyes were on the road but his expression was too intent
for just that. He was planning, she thought. Still. . .

'What next?' she asked across the silence.

He glanced across at her and grinned. 'How did you
know?'

'I'm starting to see it,' Kate confessed. 'You've plans
whirring like cogs behind your eyes.'

'Well diagnosed, Dr Harris.' The intent look
returned. 'As a matter of fact I was thinking,' he told
her. 'Wondering how long before I get public-bed
approval, and how long before I can get nursing-home
beds under way.'

'You'll build on?'

'Almost certainly.'

'Almost?' Kate mocked. 'That doesn't sound like
you. I'm wondering why you didn't start building
yesterday.'

Richard smiled absently, his attention on the winding
road. 'I do my homework properly,' he said firmly.
'Contrary to your belief, my head's not full of air
bubbles — or pipe dreams.'

Kate looked sardonically over to him. 'Really, Dr
Blair?'

'Really, Dr Harris,' he smiled. 'You'll see.'

'I'm leaving in three weeks,' she reminded him.

'As I said, we'll see,' he repeated. He glanced over
to her and slowed the car. 'What's wrong?'

Kate was staring out of the passenger window at the
house they were passing. Her green eyes narrowed in
concern. They were passing Miss Souter's.

'Stop, Richard,' she said briefly.

Richard brought the car to a halt, and then reversed
along the grassy verge to bring the car to a stop outside
Miss Souter's cottage. He frowned across at Kate.

'What is it?' he asked.

Kate was already emerging from the car, reaching
over into the back for her crutches.

'There's no smoke coming from the chimneys,' she told him. 'And the fires are Miss Souter's only form of cooking and heating.'

She fumbled awkwardly with her crutches, and then Richard was beside her, assisting her to move swiftly over the muddy verge.

The house was wrapped in silence. Nothing stirred. Richard knocked and knocked again. Leaving Kate on the front veranda, he went around to test the back door and came back shaking his head.

'Locked,' he said. 'Maybe she's gone away for a few days.'

'She hasn't anywhere to go,' Kate told him. 'And she'd let me know. She knows I worry about her. Besides. . .' She looked over at the front window. On the inside, staring plaintively out, was a little tabby cat. 'It's Meg,' Kate said. 'If she were away she wouldn't have left Meg inside.'

Richard flashed her a look under his brows and knocked again on the front door. The sound echoed eerily beyond the thick, wooden door.

'We'll have to break in,' Kate told him.

'You're that sure?'

'I'm that sure.' Kate's face had lost its colour. Over and over she was reliving the conversations she had had with the old lady about nursing homes. She had known this would happen. . .

Richard looked at the white-faced girl beside him and any hesitation he felt disappeared. Kate knew her patients, and Kate's overriding sensation was fear. He put his shoulder to the door and heaved. It didn't give.

'It looks easier than this in the movies,' he complained. Kate didn't smile.

'Should we break a window?' she asked quietly.

'I'll try the back door first.'

Two minutes later Kate heard the splintering of wood

from the back of the house. Thirty seconds after that
the front door opened and Richard appeared.

'Come in, Kate.' His voice was subdued, and Kate
knew at once that her worst fears were realised.

Miss Souter was sitting in an easy-chair in the front
parlour. At first glance she might have been staring
reflectively at the ashes of her fire. On her lap lay the
interminable knitting Kate had watched grow every
time she visited her. Her gaze, however, was sightless.
She was quite dead.

Kate touched the old cheek, and felt the cold, lifeless
skin.

'She's been dead for a while,' she said dully.

'Since last night, I'd guess,' Richard said. He looked
at Kate, his eyes seeing her pain. 'It was a good way to
go, Kate. She hasn't been in any discomfort.'

'No.' Kate straightened. 'She had pills for when the
angina was bad and she knew to phone. If she'd had
any warning she would have rung. . .' She looked dully
up at Richard. 'The phone has been working?'

Richard touched his pocket lightly. 'The phone's
been right here,' he assured her. 'She didn't ring, Kate.'

Kate closed her eyes and nodded, then opened them
as she felt something warm and soft touch her leg. She
looked down to see Meg, Miss Souter's little tabby cat,
wrapping herself listlessly around her leg. Kate lifted
her up and held her close.

'I'll look after you,' she promised, and the promise
was more to the dead Miss Souter than to the little cat.

'Why the guilt, Kate?' Richard's voice was gentle.

Kate shrugged, her hand gently stroking the cat's soft
fur. 'She was just so lonely,' she said. 'I tried to come
as often as I could. . .'

'You can't do everything.' Richard was crossing to
the phone. 'When we get my nursing-home wing set up
we'll incorporate a day centre, where we can put on a
few social activities.'

Kate smiled reluctantly. 'I hope you do,' she told him.

'I'll ring Joe,' Richard told her. 'There's not a lot we can do here.'

'No.' Kate looked sadly around.

'Has she any relatives?'

'None that I know of,' Kate told him. 'Though often relatives surface after a death. . .'

'When they stand to inherit and there's no chance of them having to do anything,' Richard finished for her, grimacing. 'I know.'

They waited at the house until Joe arrived with the ambulance. Kate cleared the kitchen of perishable food, and Richard nailed the back door closed again with tools he found in the back shed. Finally they had done all they could.

They emerged to darkness and lightly falling rain. Kate was drifting in a mist of weariness and sorrow. The old lady had been a friend as well as a patient, and Kate couldn't escape the overwhelming sensation that she had failed her. She sat listlessly in the passenger seat as Richard drove her home, aimlessly stroking the little cat.

'Will you keep him?' Richard asked gently.

'What?' Kate pulled herself back to the present with a jolt and realised Richard was talking of the cat in her arms. 'Meg?' she asked. 'Meg's a her.'

'I beg your pardon, Meg,' Richard smiled. 'Will you keep her, Dr Harris?'

'Of course I will,' Kate said softly. 'I promised.'

'Promised Meg?' Richard asked, startled.

'No.' Kate smiled ruefully. 'I promised Miss Souter. I thought you heard me.'

Richard rounded the next bend, but the car was slowing. Carefully he pulled over where a side-track led into the bush. Then, before Kate had time to respond, he had lifted the little cat from her arms and placed it carefully on to the back seat. Then he took Kate's face between his hands and his eyes held hers.

'Katy Harris,' he said firmly, 'I love you.' And he kissed her.

It was like a gift. Cutting through Kate's bleakness and despair, this kiss was a promise of a new beginning. It was a kiss between strangers, a kiss between friends and a kiss between lovers. It was all things. It was a kiss of joy.

The loneliness, the despair and the mistrust of the past few years dissolved into nothing. For this moment Kate's doubts disappeared into nothing. Worry was for tomorrow. Distrust was for tomorrow. Tonight, now, there was only Richard.

Slowly her lips parted, welcoming the taste of his mouth on hers. The last of her doubts were shoved into the background. This was her place. This was where she belonged, in the arms of the man she loved.

She did, she thought mistily. She did. She loved Richard Blair, and she wanted him so much. . .

Her hands came softly up to hold his big frame to her. The big woollen sweater was rough under her hands and she welcomed its roughness. Oh, she wanted him. She wanted all of him. Forever.

The kiss went on and on, neither wanting to break the moment. Richard's arms were holding her close, caressing the soft wool of her dress, feeling the pliant contours of her body. Kate held herself close. . .closer. Here was love. Here was her life.

Slowly they drew away. Kate was staring up at Richard as if she had never seen him before. His hands still loosely held her.

'Well, my love?' he mocked gently. 'Still doubts?'

'N-no,' she managed. 'Not now. . .'

'Just as well,' he threatened, but his voice was full of loving laughter.

Behind them, Meg miaowed plaintively as if she was

aware that the attention of these two strange human beings had been diverted. Kate gave a shaky laugh, reached over and picked her up again.

'We'd better get her home and settled,' she managed.

'It's hardly worth taking her to your place,' Richard said teasingly. 'She'll get a bit lonely.'

Kate gave a tiny gasp and buried her face in the cat's soft fur. 'Richard, don't. . .' The seeds of doubt swept back in. Just this moment, her heart was pleading. Not the future. Just this moment. Don't think about the inevitable betrayal—the pain to come. . .

'Don't rush you, my love?' Richard ran a hand down her silky hair and let it lie on her shoulder. 'How can I not?' he teased. 'I only have three weeks.' He leaned forward to turn the key in the ignition and then stopped as the phone in his pocket started to ring.

For a couple of moments he listened intently to a female voice on the other end of the line. 'OK, Janet,' he said finally. 'I'll be there in ten minutes.' He put the phone back in his pocket and started the car.

'What is it?' Kate asked. She was having trouble making her voice work.

'Chris Locket,' Richard said briefly. 'Do you know him?'

Kate thought back. 'Chris is a teenager,' she said slowly, bringing herself back to reality with an effort and remembering the history. 'He's asthmatic. He hates the medication and avoids it if possible, so his attacks are always much worse than they need to be.'

Richard sighed. 'Well, there goes an hour or so when I could have been doing much more productive things.' He flashed a smile across at Kate in the dim light of the car. 'His dad's just brought him into the hospital. Janet's giving him ventolin but she's concerned. Sounds as if I'm needed.'

'You or me,' Kate said softly.

'Well, it's me tonight,' Richard said firmly. 'Your foot should be in bed.'

He pulled to a halt outside Kate's cottage and came around to help her out. 'I think you'll find everything you need for a meal inside,' he told her. 'I asked Bella to organise something.'

'Is there anything you don't organise?' Kate asked shyly. She smiled up at him and he stooped to kiss her.

'Yes,' he said firmly. 'I don't organise an hour off right now when I desperately need it.' He put a hand on the little cat's head and scratched its ear. 'Goodnight, Meg. Look after your new mistress.'

Kate stood on the veranda and watched as his car lights disappeared down the hill. In her arms the little cat stirred and miaowed nervously. Finally, as the lights disappeared from view, Kate turned to go inside.

'Don't be scared, little cat,' she told her. 'I'm OK. You just have to learn to trust.' She put a finger to her lips where the taste of Richard's mouth was still present. 'Like me,' she whispered. 'Just for the moment I'm putting mistrust on hold. So you can too.'

CHAPTER ELEVEN

KATE woke to laughter. A kookaburra in the big gum outside her bedroom window was doing its best to wake the world with its raucous chuckle. Kate pulled back her cover, disturbing the sleepy little cat on the end of her bed, and crossed to the window.

'OK, you've succeeded,' she told the bird severely. 'Now, go away.'

The bird cocked its head to one side and surveyed the tousled girl at the window. Then it threw back its head and laughed some more.

Why did it feel so different? Kate felt about ten years younger. She pushed back the hair from her face and smiled upwards at the cackling bird.

'I don't mind waking up this morning,' she told him. 'At least. . .'

She crossed to the bed and sat down, taking the weight from her ankle. It was less tender this morning but she was still very much aware of it.

'It's true,' she told Meg, rubbing the soft fur. 'I do feel younger. I feel like a silly schoolgirl in love. . .'

She limped out to the kitchen in her nightdress. The wood stove was still warm from the night before. When Kate had walked into the house she had discovered fires lit, a stockpile of wood by the stove and her refrigerator loaded. Richard had accused her of not taking care of herself, and then had set about rectifying the situation.

Kate had eaten well, showered and gone to bed, to lie wakeful watching the shifting patterns of moonlight on the ceiling. Sleep was a long time coming and she knew why. Kate Harris desperately wanted Richard to return.

She had gone over and over in her mind how long Richard would take to care for an asthmatic teenager. Maybe all night, her head had told her. Chris had been desperately ill before, and when he was she hadn't been able to leave him. Was that why Richard hadn't returned?

She had wanted him to so much. . . 'I'm crazy,' she said to herself as she put the kettle on. 'Nothing's changed. He's just as much a spendthrift as he always was. And he's just the same as Doug. Why do I fall for men like this? Why do I have to be so damned stupid?'

Meg came sleepily out to the kitchen, yawning and showing her tiny pink tongue. Kate poured some milk into a saucer and watched the little cat lap. At least it seemed that Meg was going to settle.

'Will you come to the city with me when I go?' Kate whispered to the cat. Meg didn't look up. The question, it seemed, didn't warrant an answer.

Perhaps it didn't. The thought of leaving the valley was becoming harder and harder.

'I can't fall in love with another dreamer—a fool who spends more than he can ever earn,' Kate said harshly. Meg looked up in surprise and then reapplied herself to her breakfast. Kate stared sightlessly down and then smiled ruefully. She made herself a mug of coffee and then sat at the table in the unaccustomed warmth.

Crazy or not, it seemed she was no longer in control of her own emotions. She knew without doubt that if Richard had returned last night there could have been only one outcome.

'Perhaps it was better that he didn't,' she whispered.

The sound of a car pulling to a halt outside the house pulled Kate from her dreaming. She glanced at her wristwatch. Eight a.m. This was after the time she normally started work. Here she was, still in her nightgown, receiving Richard.

She knew even before the door opened that it was Richard. She recognised his car. She recognised his footsteps and her heart did a minor lurch in pleasure. When the door opened and she saw him, the lurch became a somersault.

'Well, well.' He stood at the open door, smiling at her, his eyes caressing the scantily clad girl. 'I came to pick up my partner to take her to work, and what do I find?'

'I'm sorry. . .' Kate was suddenly absurdly shy. She couldn't meet those gently teasing eyes. 'I'll get dressed.'

'Not yet, you won't.' In two strides Richard was across the room and had her in his arms.

Kate resisted for the whole of two seconds. Then the joy of being held by the man she loved blocked out everything else. She put her hands around his neck, held him close and lifted her face to be kissed.

Richard obliged to her entire satisfaction. When he finally ceased she was left breathless and laughing, swinging crazily in his arms.

'Richard Blair,' she said huskily, 'this is crazy.'

'I know,' he told her, his hands caressing her near-bare shoulders. He bent and kissed the smooth skin where her nightgown lay across her breasts. 'Oh, God, Kate, you're so beautiful. . .' His voice was husky with passion.

'I thought. . . I thought you might come back last night,' Kate said shyly.

Richard drew back and looked at her, his eyes fathomless. 'I couldn't,' he told her. 'I spent three hours at the hospital and after that I had overseas phone calls to make.' He hesitated. 'Would you have let me in?' he asked.

'Yes,' she said simply.

He sighed and pulled her against him. 'What about my grandiose spending, my golden girl?' he asked gently. 'How can you love a fool?'

'I make a habit of it.' Kate's voice was a whisper but her words were enough to make Richard pull away. He held her at arm's length.

'What did Doug do to you?' he demanded. 'Run up debts he couldn't pay?'

'He mortgaged everything,' Kate told him. 'Our home, my surgery, my. . .' her voice faltered '. . .my parents' home. . .'

Richard surveyed her thoughtfully. 'I'm beginning to see,' he said at last. 'If you stop work, your parents lose their home.'

'Yes.'

There was a long silence, and then Richard pulled her back against the coarse wool of his sweater. 'Kate, I'm not Doug,' he said softly. 'I won't hurt you.'

'I'm starting to think it's a risk I have to take,' Kate said quietly. She felt a tear well over to run down her cheek and burrow itself into Richard's sweater. 'But this time it will be just me taking the risks. Not my parents.'

Richard frowned down at Kate's head. 'Kate, I have never — would never — risk money other than mine. I swear. . .'

Kate shook her head against him. 'It doesn't matter.'

'It matters,' he said grimly. 'If you don't trust me. . .'

'Doesn't it only matter that I think I love you?'

Richard shook his head, his eyes not leaving her face. 'There's no love without trust,' he told her. 'Not ever.'

'But what I feel. . .'

'Is not enough, Kate. I want something more from the woman I love than emotional dependence.'

'Richard——'

He silenced her by touching her lips softly closed. Then his hands left her mouth and ran down the smooth curves of her sides, feeling the yielding of soft flesh under the thin fabric of her nightgown. As she looked up in wonder, a shudder ran through him and he pushed her away.

'Get yourself dressed, woman,' he said brusquely, his voice unsteady. 'We've work to do and if we stay here much longer I won't answer for the consequences. Have you had breakfast?'

'No. I. . .'

'Me neither. I'll cook some while you dress. Put that damned dreary skirt on again. It was a mistake to come here. . . For heaven's sake, Kate. . .'

Kate turned away. What was he saying? she wondered as she crossed to the bedroom. That he didn't want her on the terms she was offering? Hadn't she just told him she loved him? And now he was saying he wanted more.

How could she give more? How could she give the trust he demanded when Doug had destroyed it forever? The men she loved were of a type, and wishing wouldn't change it. If she could love Richard and be with him without risking financial disaster then she would. But to demand that she trust completely. . .

She couldn't, she thought sadly, as she started to dress. Not any more. Not even for Richard.

The rest of the week passed in a blur. The surgery was busy each day, much busier than Kate's clinic had been before Richard had arrived, and she realised that the town of Corrook was supporting its embryo medical centre to the fullest.

She could have done without quite as much support, and so could Richard. The hospital staff were still finding their feet, but by the end of the week they had six patients.

'It's so nice not to have to go to the city every time we need an X-ray,' Mrs Featherstone told her. She had accompanied her husband, a frail old man who had slipped and fractured his forearm.

'Who's going to put your shingle cream on now?' Kate teased her.

'We'll manage,' Archie Featherstone said with dignity. He surveyed his plaster cast ruefully. 'Though it's going to cramp our style somewhat.' He twinkled up at his wife and she giggled and blushed like a schoolgirl.

Kate was driving again, the swelling on her ankle subsiding to allow her some mobility, but she was still dependent on her crutches. As promised, Richard took care of the house calls, but the extra strain of her injured ankle made Kate fall into bed at night exhausted.

She hardly saw Richard. She kept track of his movements, as from wherever he was prescriptions came in for her to rewrite. It must be driving him nuts to be so dependent on her, she thought, writing out the twentieth for the day. And how long could it go on? Alf was showing no signs of relenting.

When they did meet they were carefully formal. Their attitude had Bella raising her eyebrows.

'What's up with you two, then? Lovers' tiff?'

'Don't be silly,' Kate told her. 'We're not lovers.'

'Then you darn well should be,' the older woman retorted. 'And don't tell me you're not nutty about him, Dr Harris, because I won't believe you.'

Kate managed to smile but shook her head. 'I'm not nutty about anyone,' she said. 'I've been married, Bella. I don't want to go down that path again.'

'You can't judge the whole barrel by one lousy apple,' Bella said sagely. 'Take my Tim. . .'

'I know,' Kate stopped her. 'You and half the women in this town have lovely marriages and caring husbands and would like nothing better than to marry me off to Richard.' She took a deep breath. 'But you should be able to see more clearly than anyone, Bella. This hospital is a financial risk. Richard's playing with fire, just like Doug did.'

'Maybe he can afford to,' Bella told her, frowning. 'Maybe he has family money. . .'

'He told me himself his mother had to struggle to keep them,' Kate said slowly. 'You'd think he would have learned. . .'

'Well, if it's a risk, it's a risk worth taking,' Bella said stoutly. 'And you should be supporting him all the way instead of criticising him.'

Kate flushed but Bella met her look squarely. 'I know it's none of my business,' she went on squarely, 'but you never get anything done if you spend your life worrying about consequences.'

'But if those consequences hurt others. . .'

Kate broke off as the phone rang on the surgery desk. Bella cast another worried look up at Kate and then picked up the receiver. A patient walked in the door and their time of confidence was at an end.

Perhaps it was just as well, Kate told herself. Bella couldn't help her. No one could make Richard into something he wasn't—dependable, trustworthy and solid. Her heart twisted within her as she acknowledged what her head was telling her.

'I hope you're advertising for another partner,' she told Richard as they finished work for the evening. 'I'll only be here for the rest of the month.'

Richard looked at her for a long moment and then turned away. Her words obviously didn't warrant a reply.

On Friday Kate finished work early and made her way to the little church on the hill behind the town. She was one of half a dozen people at Miss Souter's funeral, and the only friend who attended the graveyard.

The old lady had been a loner, Kate knew, but the coldness of the farewell chilled her. Had there ever been a family? Had there ever been people who loved her?

She stood in the bleak little graveyard for a long time after the service was read, trying to make sense of the lonely life. She had been fond of the old woman. Why hadn't others?

There were no answers. Dusk was falling as she turned to limp back to her car. As she neared the gate of the graveyard a big silver Mercedes pulled to a halt and Richard emerged.

'I thought you'd be here,' he said softly. 'Bella said you'd cut the book off early.'

'I had to,' Kate said simply. 'She had. . . There was no one else.'

Richard looked over to where a single wreath of wild flowers lay on the newly covered grave. 'Yours?' he asked.

'From Meg.' Kate managed a smile.

Richard placed a hand under her arm and supported her on the rough ground to the car. Kate was trying to manage without her crutches and finding the going difficult.

'Thank you,' she said stiffly, lowering herself into her car.

'Come and have dinner with me, Kate,' Richard said quietly. Then as she opened her mouth to speak he pre-empted her. 'Not at my place,' he said. 'At the pub.'

'I thought you didn't like the pub.'

'Only when I want to talk business. And I don't want to talk business tonight.'

Kate hesitated. She shouldn't. . .

The thought of going back to her cold little house and having a lonely tea was suddenly as bleak as the graveyard. Richard's eyes were on her face, watchful and waiting. She flashed a look up at him and caught an expression she didn't understand. It was as if he was as confused as she was.

'OK,' she smiled suddenly. The thought of the pub, full of warmth and talk, laughter and people, was infinitely appealing. 'But just for an hour.'

'I wouldn't want to impinge on your precious time any longer,' he told her.

The meal was just what Kate needed. The pub was crowded with a Friday-night crowd out to shake off the week's work. Most of the locals were farmers who came in after milking, and the aroma of the dairy was unmistakable. Kate wrinkled her nose as she walked in the door.

'You'd think they'd have a bath,' she whispered to Richard and he grinned.

'What, and waste good drinking time?'

There was a vast fire blazing in the hearth. The waitress showed them to a table beside it, beaming her welcome.

'We wondered when we'd see our new doctor in here,' she beamed. 'And welcome back, Dr Harris. The boss says to tell you drinks are on him tonight.'

It was like a welcome home after the grim funeral — a welcome back to life and laughter. Despite her awareness of the man beside her, Kate settled back to enjoy herself.

It seemed that was what Richard intended too. Miraculously, for once, the phone in his pocket was quiet and they had an uninterrupted meal. Kate had specified an hour, but her limit sped past unnoticed. She was relaxed, she was warm and she was happy.

'Do you come here often?' Richard asked as another of the locals stopped to greet them and then moved on.

'I come here to eat when. . .'

'When your house gets too lonely,' Richard finished for her, his eyes a question. 'Am I right, Kate?'

Kate smiled and shrugged her shoulders. 'Could be,' she said lightly.

'That's not going to change unless you let your barriers down,' he told her.

'Leave myself open for betrayal again, you mean?' Kate stared into her glass of wine, swirling it around in the glass.

Richard's hand came over the table and caught hers. The pressure on her fingers increased until she was forced to look up. 'What makes you so sure betrayal is inevitable?' he demanded.

'I didn't say it was inevitable,' Kate told him seriously. She met his eyes and then wished she hadn't. It was like drowning. . . The warmth, the light and the laughter were combining to make her feel light-headed. She pushed the glass of wine away from her. She didn't want any more. Half a glass and already. . .

It wasn't the wine, she knew. It was not this place, or the warmth, or the people. It was this man, sitting before her, his eyes uttering a challenge she could not meet. Love me, they were saying. Trust me. Give yourself to me. . .

She averted her head and made a half-hearted attempt to tug away her hand. Richard's grip tightened.

'I have to go home,' she said faintly. 'Meg needs feeding.'

'Does your house run to coffee?' Richard demanded.

'I. . .' Once again Kate met those eyes and once again she was lost. 'Yes,' she said weakly.

'So be it,' Richard said, rising. 'Coffee at your place.'

'I don't think——'

'That's right,' Richard cut in on her doubts. 'Just keep on not thinking. It seems to me every time you let your head rule you say something insulting.' He ushered her expertly through the crowded room before she had time to answer.

Kate's little car was parked beside the main entrance. Richard opened the driver's door for her, and then, to her surprise, walked around and sank on to the passenger seat.

'You're chauffeuring, Dr Harris,' he told her. 'I've had one too many beers.'

Kate did a quick recall in her head and cast a suspicious glance across at him. 'You only had two,' she said slowly. 'And I thought they were light beer.'

'I know when I shouldn't drive,' Richard told her. 'And tonight I definitely shouldn't drive. I'll walk home later.'

'Walk. . .' Kate's voice was near a squeak. 'It's nearly two miles.'

'It'll sober me up.'

'And if you're called?'

Richard smiled. Leaning over, he placed the mobile phone carefully in her lap. 'I counted your wine consumption, Dr Harris. After only half a glass, you are definitely on call.'

Kate tried to smile. 'I'll drop you at your place,' she said.

'No.'

'What do you mean, no?' she snapped.

'Negative. I'm going to feed Meg.' Richard sat back, arms folded, in the attitude of one who had come to the only righteous course of action and was going to stick with it to the end. Despite her confusion Kate was betrayed into a giggle.

'You sound as though you think I'll starve her.'

'You can't be too careful,' Richard told her. 'And I never returned Miss Souter's sponge-cake plate. I owe her a debt.'

'So you'll repay it by checking up on me.'

'Something like that,' he admitted.

Kate cast him a suspicious look, but Richard's expression was one of benign indifference. He sat, immovable.

'I'll drive you home after you've checked,' she muttered.

'As you like.'

There was nothing for it but to swallow her reservations and take the man home.

CHAPTER TWELVE

MEG greeted them at the door, purring her ecstasy at having human companionship once more. Richard swung the door open, ushered Kate indoors and then lifted the little cat into his arms.

'I might have known,' he said direfully. 'This place is freezing again. How can a cat survive in Arctic terrain like this?'

'Cats are tougher than you think,' Kate snapped.

Richard raised his eyebrows. 'Touchy, aren't we, Dr Harris?'

'Yes,' Kate said shortly, crossing to the kitchen.

'Why?'

'Bcause I don't like being forced to spend time with you.'

'No one did any forcing,' Richard said quietly. He placed the little cat carefully on the kitchen floor before the saucer of milk Kate was pouring. 'You were happy for me to come back for coffee.'

'I wasn't. . .'

'Which part of you, Kate? Your head or your heart.'

Kate stared up at him and then turned back to the bench. She lifted the kettle to fill it but her fingers refused to work the way she wanted. She fumbled with the tap and Richard's arms came around her. One strong hand held the kettle, the other twisted the tap on and then off. He moved aside to place the kettle on the stove and then came back to where she was standing. Kate hadn't moved. She was still standing facing the sink.

His hands spanned her waist, pulling her back so that her body was curved into his. His lips met the warmth of the skin on the back of her neck, moving aside the errant wisps of hair as he kissed her.

Kate's eyes filled with helpless tears. How could she fight this feeling? How could she fight this man?

'You don't want to fight, do you, Kate?' Richard murmured. 'You want me just as much as I want you.'

Yes! her body was screaming at her. Yes. . . Her injured ankle was jelly beneath her and the other wasn't much better. Her back curved into the hard maleness of his body and her heart melted in love and desire.

'Kate. . .'

'Y-yes. . .' If Richard hadn't been close he would never have heard her shaken whisper, but he was close enough.

'Kate, all you have to do is let go. All you have to do is trust. . .'

Kate closed her eyes and gave a tiny sob. It wasn't of pain, though. Her head had lost any fight she was trying to maintain long since. Trust, her heart screamed at her. This man is right. This man is so unlike Doug that the comparison is laughable. This man loves you, and to hold qualms any longer will endanger that love.

'How much do you owe your parents?' Richard said slowly, his lips moving on her neck. Kate stiffened. She made a half-hearted attempt to pull away but his hands tightened. He pulled her around to face him, holding her at arm's length.

'You have to tell me, Kate,' he said softly. 'You have to trust me, or nothing can grow between us. Where there's no trust, there's no love.'

'But I. . .'

'No buts. Tell me, Kate.' He bent and kissed her on the lips, a feather-light kiss that was the promise of things to come. 'All you have to do is let go,' he told her. 'The armour's had its uses. It's time to take it off.'

Kate stared helplessly up at him. He made it all sound so easy.

And suddenly it was. His eyes told her that. They were watching her with kindness, compassion and love. He wanted her love, but he needed trust. His love was a gift, and the gift had a price. And the price was nothing. Trust. . . Somehow, it was already given.

She sighed, a sigh that let out all the pain she had been holding in since Doug had walked out on her two years ago. This man had nothing to do with Doug. Whatever Doug had done could not be repeated. Not by Richard. Not by her love. . .

His eyes still held her, waiting for what she would give. And she gave it. Leaning against the comforting wool of his sweater, her face hidden in its folds, she told him all that Doug had done to her. She told him of her debts. She told him things she had never told anyone, things that left her feeling vulnerable and exposed to the world. She didn't worry. Those things were safe with him.

And when she was finished Richard was silent for a long time. They stood, motionless, while the kettle blasted steam across the kitchen and the little cat wound itself around their legs looking for its next course.

'What's next, my Kate?' Richard asked slowly, placing a finger under her chin to force her tear-drenched eyes up to meet his. 'You trust me with this knowledge. . . Do you trust me with yourself?'

Her eyes said it all. There was no need to answer.

Richard pulled her to him and kissed her. The little cat was forgotten. There was only each other.

The smell of burning metal drew them apart. Richard released her and looked around. The kettle was no longer boiling. From the base came a threatening hiss. He swore and moved to take it from the stove. Kate watched, and then turned away to open a can of cat food. As she finished, Richard's arms came around her once more.

'Domestic chores finished?'

'Where's my coffee?' she teased him.

'Coffee's off,' he said gravely. 'On account of a ruddy great hole beneath the kettle.'

'My best kettle!'

'I'll buy you another,' he said grandly. He kissed her lightly on the forehead. 'You won't accuse me of gross extravagance if I do, will you?'

Kate smiled ruefully. 'I'm sorry,' she whispered. 'It's just. . .'

Richard closed her lips with his fingers. 'No more doubts,' he said firmly. 'Not tonight, my love.'

Then, suddenly, she was in his arms, and he was striding across the living-room to the bedroom beyond. He closed the door with his foot, his eyes laughing down at the girl in his arms.

'I don't mind cats,' he said. 'But even Miss Souter would have to agree they have their place.'

'Miss Souter would be shocked to the core at such goings-on,' Kate whispered. Her arms tightened around Richard's neck. 'Richard, I'm not. . . I'm not protected.'

He eyed her sardonically, the twinkle lurking deep behind his eyes. 'Fear not, my love,' he grinned. 'Some of us have had forethought.'

'Richard Blair. . .' Kate gasped and wriggled in his clasp. It was futile. The clasp tightened. 'Did you mean to seduce me tonight?'

'Of course I did,' Richard said equably. 'I've been planning it all week.'

'You. . .' She gazed up at him in indignation. He laughed down at her and her indignation dissipated into a chuckle. 'Oh, Richard. . .'

'Oh, Kate,' he mocked. And then the laughter died slowly from his eyes and he bent to kiss her. 'Oh, my lovely Kate.'

Then, suddenly, they were on the bed and Richard was lifting Kate's garments from her one by one.

'You know, I'm getting quite attached to this skirt,' he told her as he loosened the zip.

'Leave it on, then,' Kate teased him.

The zip was pulled to its limit. The skirt somehow was off, and airborne to the other side of the room. 'Like the cat, it has its place,' Richard told her, his hands moving gently over her soft skin. 'And that place is not here. Oh, God, Kate, you are so beautiful.'

He stood back from the bed, soaking in her nakedness, wanting to know each part of her from a distance. Then his clothes too were flung aside and Kate's quivering body melted to his nakedness. Skin met skin and it was all Kate could do not to cry out in ecstasy.

And when he took her it was right. It was as it should be — two bodies moulding to each other as two halves of a whole. They moved together in perfect rhythm and their peak came as the crescendo of a rapture Kate had never known before and could not believe she would know again. She held his body to hers as if she couldn't bear ever to leave him. Tears were coursing down her face and her body was dissolving in a mist of joy.

Richard traced a teardrop down her cheek. 'Tears, my Kate?' he asked tenderly.

'I can't help it,' she sobbed. 'I'm so happy. And I never deserved this. I. . .'

He silenced her with a kiss, and the kiss went on and on forever. It only lessened as they drifted into sleep.

Towards dawn Kate woke. The first weak dawn rays were filtering through the window to lie over the figures curved into each other on the bed. Kate's body was moulded to Richard's, her back warm against his chest. The feel of him was enough to send a shiver of pleasure down her spine. Richard's eyes opened and his arms tightened around her.

'Too early to rise, my Kate,' he told her sleepily. He put a hand out to inspect his watch. 'Six a.m. and

Saturday morning. No surgery this morning, and no calls all night.'

'Don't push your luck,' Kate whispered. The feel of his skin on hers was sending shards of pleasure through her. It was all she could do not to purr, she thought. 'Boasting of no calls is the surest way I know of getting one in the next five minutes.'

'We can't come anyway,' Richard said, his hand stroking the flatness of her belly and then moving to feel her inner warmth. Kate gave a gasp of pleasure at the feel of him. She writhed in his grasp and his hands moved more urgently. 'We'd have to tell them we're otherwise engaged.'

'But we. . .we're not doing anything,' Kate stammered.

'Aren't we just?' Richard demanded.

Afterwards Kate slept again. When she woke he was gone.

She stared stupidly at the empty pillow beside her while her mind tried to work out where he was. It was as if a conjurer had magicked him away. You've had enough pleasure, the conjurer would have decreed. Off with you. And Richard had vanished in a puff of smoke.

Kate blinked. She was losing her mind, she decided. She turned sleepily to look at her bedside table and shot upright. Ten-thirty. Even without a surgery there was a ward-round and any urgent cases to be seen. She slid guiltily from the bed and padded through to the kitchen.

Meg greeted her with joy, leaving her spot on the chair by the fire to miaow around her legs. Kate looked around with amazement. The fire was lit, her breakfast laid out, the little cat's bowl filled and a note was propped against the cereal bowl. It said:

Someone has to do the work of the world, and you need your beauty sleep more than me. Love you.

As a first love letter it lacked a certain dignity, but Kate held it to her cheek for a moment just the same. 'It'll do,' she told Meg happily.

What had changed in the last twenty-four hours she didn't know. All she knew was that Richard had demanded her trust and she had given it to him.

'Am I being stupid, Meg, girl?' she demanded as she poured herself coffee from the pot on the stove. 'If I am, it's too late. I'm in love right up to my ears and back down again.'

Kate breakfasted slowly and then ran herself a long bath. The day stretched before her deliciously, revolving around and around the thought of Richard. 'He loves me,' she said over and over to herself. The issue of trust had receded to almost nothing. She pushed away the thought of Richard's massive spending spree as something she no longer had the strength to face. If she looked at it closely the seed of doubt started again, and she desperately didn't want to doubt. Not Richard. Not her love. . .

An hour later there was no sign of Richard. Kate glanced at her watch. She should go down to the hospital. Even if Richard was doing the rounds, there were patients she should see. Besides, he might be there. . . She dressed casually in jeans and a big sweater, and turned her little car down the track.

She slowed as she neared Richard's house. Looking up the track, she half expected the Mercedes to be in the drive. She frowned to herself, wondering what Richard would have done. He must have walked to the house and rung Pete for a taxi. If he'd rung from Kate's place, half the town would know where he had spent the night before the taxi even arrived.

He'll be down at the hospital, she told herself. Even so, her car slowed further and she looked up at the smoke coming from Richard's chimney. He had been home. . . Then a movement at one of the windows caught her eye. Someone was home. . .

Kate frowned. Surely Richard would have caught a taxi down to the hotel to collect his car? She turned her little car into the drive. She was going to have to check that he didn't need a lift down.

Ten seconds later she was limping up the front step of Richard's house. As she raised her hand to knock the door opened inwards. A girl appeared, blonde, tousle-haired and dressed in a loose housecoat. She was small and slender and almost startlingly good-looking, despite her lack of make-up. She smiled welcomingly at Kate and held out her hand.

'Don't tell me,' she said warmly. 'Let me guess. You're Dr Harris.'

'I. . .yes. . .' Kate stammered. She must have sounded as stunned as she felt because the other girl burst into laughter.

'You're nearly as surprised as Richard, I'll bet.' She was grasping Kate's limp hand. 'I'm Christy Blair.'

'Christy Blair. . .'

'Come on in.' Christy held the door wide and Kate moved inside. Scattered over the hall was a mountain of luggage. Christy saw Kate's gaze and grinned. 'Well, I don't travel light,' she smiled. 'Not when I'm here to stay.' She grimaced, holding the housecoat closer. 'Though Richard might have told me to expect this cold. I thought Australia was supposed to be hot.'

'Not south in winter,' Kate said mechanically. She looked down at Christy's hand. On her left hand was a wide, golden wedding-band. 'You. . .you've moved here to be with Richard.'

'Well, yes,' Christy said, as though it was something Kate should have expected. 'Mind, I wasn't coming quite as soon as this. Richard wanted to be settled before I came over, and there was our house full of furniture and belongings in England I was supposed to be disposing of. But he rang last week and said he needed me now. . .' She spread her hands expressively. 'What girl can refuse a plea like that? I left the rest of our business in England in the hands of an agent and came.'

'Today. . .'

'Today,' Christy told her. 'My plane got in at some horrible hour last night. I caught the train and then a taxi.' She smiled. 'I wanted to surprise Richard, you see. I've missed him so much.'

'I suppose you must have,' Kate said bleakly. She searched for something more to say. Her throat felt like sandpaper and the beginning of tears were pricking behind her eyes. 'Welcome to Australia,' she managed. She turned. 'I'm sorry I can't stay. I'm on my way down to the hospital. . .'

'Richard's down there,' Christy smiled. She held out her hand again. 'I'm really pleased to meet you, Kate. Richard's told me so much about you.'

Kate looked at her blindly for a long moment and then tried to smile. The way to the door seemed endless.

Christy came out to the veranda and waved as Kate backed out of the drive. It was all Kate could do to drive away. Don't let me cry, she was pleading with herself. Don't let me cry. Christy's nice. She doesn't need to know what a fink she's married to.

Married. . . The word went over and over in her head, thumping intolerably like a physical pain. The vision of Doug the night she had confronted him with his infidelity slammed back into her head—and the girl. . . She had seen her once, at the airport, a lovely laughing girl gazing adoringly up at Kate's husband.

'Like me and Christy's husband,' Kate whispered bitterly.

Somehow she managed to get her car home. She

parked outside her little cottage, put her head down on the steering-wheel and wept.

Afterwards she was calmer. Pain gave way, firstly to a cold, desolate emptiness and then to anger. How could he do it? What had he hoped to achieve?

A one-night stand before Christy had appeared? Or had he hoped to continue the relationship after Christy's arrival? He'd even said he wanted to marry her. What a joke. And she'd fallen for it, hook, line and sinker.

How can he have lied so convincingly? she demanded of herself.

'Easily,' she replied out loud, her voice so savage that the little cat on the hearth decided she'd like to go outside for a while. Kate didn't notice her leave. 'He runs risks, Richard Blair. He takes chances, with other peoples' lives as well as his own.'

All she wanted to do was to get away from the valley. She wanted to pack her bags and run. Only the thought of the hospital stopped her.

'The people of the valley need this hospital,' she told herself bitterly. 'It won't be me who destroys the dream. I'll stay until my month is up, even if it kills me. . .'

Later, she found the calm to drive down once again to the hospital. Richard's Mercedes was in the drive of his home as she flashed past but she didn't slow. At least he wasn't still in the hospital. She could do her ward-round in peace.

It was almost soothing to step back into her medicine. Medicine, for Kate, was a balm. Here she was needed, doing a job where she could drive the mess of her personal life from her mind. She mechanically checked Bert King's legs, and re-dressed them. While listening to the old man's myriad complaints about his damned-fool relatives who, she gathered, had been neglecting his chooks, she could almost block Richard from her mind.

Almost, but not quite. The pain remained, a dull, desolate ache. She had never felt so alone. She rose to go, and as she reached the hospital entrance Richard's car pulled into the car park.

Kate stared blindly across at him. She almost expected him to ignore her, but he waved, smiled and came across. His eyes twinkled down at her in the way she had grown to love. In his checked open-necked shirt and jeans he looked every inch a farmer on holiday. The wind ruffled his fair hair and Kate caught her breath at the sight of him. She loved him so much. . . She couldn't believe she was such a fool. . .

'Kate. . .'

'Yes,' she said icily.

He stopped and stared down at her, his brow creasing into a frown. 'What is it, my Kate?' he said softly.

'I am not your Kate,' Kate managed. 'I was fool enough to think I loved you. I'm not fool enough to continue the relationship now.'

The smile faded from Richard's face. He gripped her shoulders and held her hard. 'What is this, Kate? What's going on?'

Kate shoved his hands away. 'You must take me for an unprincipled tart,' she said savagely. 'I met Christy this morning. If you think I'm going to keep up a relationship with you while your wife is in the same valley. . .' Her voice broke on a sob. 'While you have a wife at all. . .'

'A wife. . .?' Richard was looking at her as if she had taken leave of her senses.

'A wife.' Kate put a hand up to brush away tears angrily. 'I knew you were just like Doug. If you think I'll stand by while you cheat on your wife. . . If you think——'

'I'm not married.' Richard's voice was like a douche of cold water, slicing across Kate's rising hysteria.

Kate stared up at him, her tears checked. His face was closed and cold. His eyes held only anger.

'B-but Christy. . .'

'Christy is my sister. She arrived this morning from England.'

'But. . .' Kate swallowed a sob. 'She. . .she's married. . .'

'She's no more married than I am.' Richard's voice was coldly contemptuous. 'I thought you'd decided to trust me, Dr Harris. It seems I've been the fool.'

'Richard. . .' Kate stared up at him in horror. If what he was saying was true. . . What had she done? Richard's eyes held nothing but cold disdain.

'Richard. . .'

'Dr Blair?' A nurse had appeared on the steps leading into the hospital. She looked across to the two doctors standing below and hesitated, as if sensing something wrong. Richard turned to her.

'Yes, Sister?'

'Mrs Mannaway. . . Sophie's mum is on the phone. She'd like to speak to you. Shall I tell her to ring back?'

'I'll come now.' Richard didn't look back at Kate. He strode swiftly up the steps without a backward glance.

Kate stood as if struck. Her face turned from white to crimson and back to white again. Richard's face had told her, more clearly than any words, that she had killed any love he felt for her. He had demanded her trust and she had responded with the worst of all accusations. She closed her eyes, willing the ground to open beneath her feet. It didn't happen. When she opened them, she was still in the hospital car park and she was still alone.

'For the rest of my life,' she whispered. 'Oh, Kate, you stupid, stupid fool.'

CHAPTER THIRTEEN

SOMEHOW Kate managed to survive the next few days. She worked in a cloud of pain and despair, willing her time to end so that she could leave this valley forever.

Richard was coldly courteous and totally aloof. Kate hardly saw him. Even the tenuous link of signing his scripts no longer existed. Another major change had taken place in the medical services for the valley. Christy Blair had set up shop as a pharmacist in a room behind the hospital.

'I couldn't believe my luck,' she told Kate when Kate met her in the hospital on her first day's work. Christy was looking cute and efficient in a white dispensing overall and bright red stockings. She was literally bouncing with happiness. 'When Mum died both Richard and I decided to emigrate. I had a good job, though, and we weren't sure what opportunities there were for pharmacists over here. When Richard rang it was all I could do to stop long enough to pack.'

Kate attempted a smile. Christy's cheerfulness and good humour were infectious and the hospital staff were warming to her.

'Can you make a living here, though?' Kate asked. 'With Alf still here?'

'Alf's told everyone he's retiring,' Christy grinned. 'When Richard complained to the pharmaceutical board about him not filling prescriptions, they contacted him and he was unwise enough to tell them to do their worst because he was retiring anyway. Therefore there was no objection at all to me starting up. And I can make do on a limited distribution until he does retire. It's such a marvellous opportunity.'

Kate smiled again. Her smile these days wasn't quite reaching her eyes and the other girl noticed.

'Kate, Richard and you. . .' she said hesitatingly. 'I thought from what Richard said on the phone when I was still in England that there was something between you. And all Richard will say now is that you thought we were married and he'd thought. . .' She hesitated and placed a hand on Kate's arm. 'Kate, I'd die if I thought I'd mucked things up between you.'

'You didn't,' Kate said slowly. She was standing in the little pharmacy waiting for Christy to prepare a script. There were advantages in having the pharmacist on hospital premises.

'You didn't think we were married?'

'I did for a moment,' Kate admitted. 'Your ring. . .'

Christy glanced down at her now bare finger and laughed ruefully. 'I was hoping I didn't meet a hunk on the plane,' she laughed. 'It was my mother's wedding-ring. I was darned if I was going to trust it to my luggage for the trip, and that was the only finger it fitted.' She looked up to Kate. 'I would have hated to lose it,' she told her.

Kate sighed. All things were now clear.

'Richard hadn't told you about me?' Christy said softly, watching Kate's face.

'No.' Kate picked up the bottle of tablets Christy had given her and fingered them. 'But then, we haven't talked very much. I. . .we don't know each other very well.'

'And now you're leaving.' Christy's smile slipped. 'It does seem a shame. Richard says he's advertising for a locum to start next week.'

'He can't start soon enough,' Kate told her.

'You're so unhappy?'

Kate flashed her a look. Despite her exuberant personality, Christy Blair saw too much.

'It is a shame you and Richard aren't hitting it off,'

Christy continued. 'For just a little while when I first
arrived he seemed so happy—so much younger than I
remembered.'

'Richard's always happy,' Kate said shortly. 'Life
seems a joke to him.'

Christy frowned and looked thoughtfully at the other
girl. 'That's not the way I'd describe my Richard,' she
said thoughtfully. 'He's always been the one to carry
the weight of the world on his shoulders. . .'

'Richard!'

'Richard,' said Christy decisively. 'You know, he's
been supporting my mother for years, and he scrimped
and saved to help put me through pharmacy school.
Life's been a serious business for a long time now.' She
met Kate's unbelieving look. 'You know, the Mercedes
he's driving is the first car he's ever owned. He wouldn't
have one in London. He wouldn't do anything. Money
was so tight. Until this year, when I graduated, and
Mum died. . .'

'He's more than making up for it now,' Kate said
bitterly.

'I know,' Christie smiled. 'And it's great to see.
When Mum died we had a letter from some solicitors
in Australia. It seemed there was some money held in
trust from my father's estate for the two of us.' She
shrugged. 'Rather a lot, actually,' she admitted. 'It
came from my grandfather's estate, but it seems my
grandfather fought with my father and intended my
parents never to find out about it.' She grinned. 'I spent
heaps of mine immediately on riotous living and I've
riotous living left to enjoy, though it will help if Alf
agrees to sell his pharmacy. Richard paced the living-
room for days, though, and then announced he was
investing the lot of it back into Australia, into something worthwhile. No riotous living for our Richard.'
She wrinkled her nose and laughed. 'I was so pleased

when I saw the Mercedes. He should get some pleasure from it.'

Kate almost gaped at her. Richard. . . Careful. Conscientious. Caring. Totally trustworthy. . .

'Is anything wrong, Kate?' Christy demanded. 'You've gone an awful colour.'

Kate shook her head numbly and turned away. Her world was reeling about her and she felt almost sick with dizziness. Where had her stupid, mistrustful head led her?

'To lose my love,' she whispered beneath her breath. 'Oh, Richard. . .'

'I'd so hoped there was something between you,' Christy said sadly. 'He sounded so excited on the phone. And he's so darned cautious with women. For so long there's been Mum and me dependent on him, and his medicine taking every waking hour. . .'

Cautious. . . Christy was talking about a different man, Kate decided. How could this be the same man who had proposed within a week of meeting her?

It no longer mattered. Kate thanked Christy and turned back into the hospital corridor with a heavy heart. If she could erase time. . .unsay words. . .

There was nothing she could do. The damage was done. The look Richard cast her as he passed her in the corridor was cold and disdainful and Kate died a little each time she saw him. He had given his love so swiftly, and she had repaid him with bitter distrust. Now it seemed she had killed that love forever.

She spent her final week packing up her meagre belongings in the little cottage. She had arranged a job with a locum service in Melbourne and wanted to be gone on Friday as soon as surgery ended.

'I've a locum coming on Monday,' Richard told her brusquely as he met her on the hospital steps midweek. 'He'll keep the hospital going until I can find a replacement.'

'I'm glad,' Kate said quietly. Impulsively she put out her hand. 'Richard. . .'

'Is there any other business you wish to discuss, Dr Harris?' he asked coldly. Kate flinched.

'No.' She turned away.

By Friday she was as close to breaking as she could possibly get. It was all she could do to function in the surgery — to keep her mind on the problems her patients were presenting. It didn't help matters that many of the patients were in tears.

'We're going to miss you,' Bella told her, sniffing dolefully into her handkerchief as Kate finished seeing her last patient. 'Oh, Kate. . .'

'Are there any house calls?' Kate asked quietly.

'Dr Blair's doing all of them this evening.' Bella emerged from her handkerchief. 'He said you wouldn't have time. Mr McGuinness asked you to pop in, though. He said it's not medical but he wants to see you.'

Kate nodded. The local solicitor was a fussy little man in his seventies. She'd been looking after his hernia and his gallstones and his high blood-pressure since she arrived in Corrook, and she would miss him. . . As she would miss all of them, she thought sadly. The elderly solicitor no doubt wanted her to have a farewell sherry with him. She would have to find the time. . .

First, though, she had to say goodbye to Richard. She owed him that courtesy. All the same, it took all the courage she possessed to walk across to his door and knock.

'Come in.' Richard's voice was brusque and business-like. Kate hesitated and then opened the door. Richard's head was bent over his day sheet. He didn't look up.

'I'm going now,' Kate said softly.

'Done your day sheets?'

Kate flushed. 'My work is up to date,' she said stiffly.

'The locum should be able to walk in and take over with no trouble.'

'While you walk off with no regrets.'

Kate bit her lips. 'There are regrets,' she said quietly. 'Any number of them. I'm sorry, Richard. I'm sorry for misjudging you.'

He looked up then, his eyes hard and still. 'I wish that were enough, Kate,' he said softly. 'I wish a simple sorry could wipe the slate clean. But it doesn't, does it?'

Kate shook her head sadly. 'No, Richard.'

It was true. The scars of her marriage and her betrayal were still there and would surface over and over. Richard deserved something more than a scarred and tainted love.

'Goodbye,' she whispered.

'Kate. . .'

Kate hesitated and looked questioningly across at the man behind the desk. With three swift strides he had risen and was around to where she stood. Grasping her shoulders, he pulled her to him and kissed her hard on the mouth. It was a brutal, punishing kiss, a kiss of anger and of pain.

'Goodbye, my Kate,' he said harshly, and pushed her out of the door.

Kate was left, staring at the closed door, the taste of salt tears on her lips.

Mr McGuinness lived behind his office, three doors from the surgery. Kate stood outside on the pavement for a moment until she was sure that the tears had stopped, and then walked the few steps to the solicitor's office. He had obviously been waiting for her, ushering her into the front office. Kate was vaguely surprised. He usually showed her into his living-room. Still, the sherry was already poured. The elderly man handed her a glass and cleared his throat.

'I suppose you're wondering why I summoned you

here this evening,' he began. His tone was slightly portentous and Kate's curiosity grew. It seemed this was a business call.

It definitely was. 'I've hurried this business through because I knew you were leaving,' the solicitor told her. 'And I thought you might well have a use for this in your new life.' He picked up a slip of paper from the desk and handed it to her. Kate looked blankly down and then looked again. It was a cheque, made out for an almost staggering amount of money.

'But. . .but. . . I don't understand,' she complained. She stared again at the amount written on the cheque and sat down hard. The cheque was made out to Dr Kate Harris. She looked up to find the solicitor beaming down on her.

'It's not often such a pleasant duty comes my way,' he smiled. 'And may I say that it couldn't happen to a nicer young lady?'

Kate laid the cheque carefully down on the desk. Her hand was shaking and she was having trouble balancing the sherry with the other. 'Would you mind explaining?' she asked.

'Of course, my dear,' the solicitor beamed. 'It's Miss Souter's estate. Not all of it, of course. There's still the proceeds from the sale of the cottage, and there are still some shares to be sold. But I've done my best to accumulate as much as I could for you to take with you.'

Kate sat silent. The old solicitor sipped his sherry and waited. The girl needed time to recover from such a shock as this.

'I can't take it,' Kate said at last. 'It's not ethical. She was my patient.'

'I thought you'd say that,' Ben McGuinness said firmly. 'I've checked. There are no relatives at all as far as we can discover, and we've done a fairly comprehensive search. She was the only child of only children.

And her will states unequivocally that she leaves everything to you. She made it out in this very office, and
she had me check that you would be permitted to keep
it before she wrote it in. It's all very clear.' He pursed
his lips. 'Mavis Souter was a very lonely old woman,'
he went on. 'You gave her much pleasure, my dear.
Your legacy is deserved.'

'Oh, it's not,' Kate said, distressed. She stood and
paced the floor. 'How can I take this?'

'You have no choice,' the solicitor said gently. 'It's
legally yours. If you wish to rip up the cheque, that's
up to you, but the amount will be transferred to your
bank account anyway. It's your money, my dear.' He
smiled and laid a hand on her shoulder. 'And it was
Miss Souter's wish that you enjoy it.'

'As she didn't,' Kate said bitterly. She looked down
again at the amount on the cheque. 'She had no
enjoyment from this money at all. How could she have
so much and be so alone. . .? She could have done
anything.'

'And been just as lonely,' Ben McGuinness told her.

Kate left the office in a daze. She couldn't drive to
Melbourne tonight, she decided. It was almost dark
already, and she felt heartsick and confused. One more
night in the valley, she decided. She would leave first
thing in the morning. She looked again at the cheque in
her hand and then slipped it into her blouse pocket.
Time also in the morning to decide what to do with
this.

Kate drove home slowly, conscious of the feeling of
unreality surrounding her and careful not to let it
transfer itself to her driving. Light rain was falling and
the roads were slippery and treacherous. It would be
good to spend one more night in the valley, she
thought, even if her house was empty and cold. One
more night in the place where she would leave her
heart. . .

What on earth should she do with Miss Souter's legacy? It wasn't hers, she decided. It was Miss Souter's right to leave it where she liked, but Kate knew that if she hadn't been Miss Souter's doctor then she wouldn't have inherited. It was as simple as that. She might legally stand to inherit but morally she had no rights at all. So what could she do? She could hardly hand the money back.

Too many things crowding into her tired mind. . . Too many things. . . Maybe she needed to get right away from this place to see things in perspective. She rounded a bend in the road—and slammed her brakes on hard. Someone—a figure in a dark coat and hat with rain dripping from his clothing and a lantern waving in his hand—was signalling for her to stop.

Kate pulled over to the side of the road and opened the window. She recognised the sodden figure. It was Paul Manuel, the farmer whose land adjoined the road.

'What's wrong, Paul?' she asked.

'Oh, Doc.' Paul's broad face showed relief as he realised who was in the car. 'That was quick.'

'What was quick?' Kate pulled open the door of the car, grabbed her coat and emerged into the rain.

'The missus just went up to call the ambulance. I thought you musta. . .'

'No. I'm on my way home. Tell me what's wrong.'

Paul wasted no time talking. He grabbed her hand and led her to where the road met the steep embankment, falling away to the creek running beside the road. Kate stopped in horror. A car was lying pinned by the trees a few yards below the road. It was on its side. All Kate could see was the wheels, facing the sky.

'There's someone in it?' Kate was already scrambling down the bank, cursing her weak ankle which held her back.

'Dorrie Clarke,' Paul told her. He was right behind her, holding the lantern high. 'She's been in Melbourne all week with Ron—you know Ron got that cancer cut off his back this week. She musta been tired and relaxed when she got near home. Missed the bend.'

'Only Dorrie?'

'I think so,' Paul said dubiously. 'No kids in the car. I had a bit of a look round in case they were thrown out but couldn't see no one.'

Kate had reached the car. She stared at it helplessly. Trees blocked the front and rear windows. The only access was through the side-door, up high. The other side was hard on the ground. Behind the precariously balanced car was a drop of some twenty feet down to the creek below.

'How do you know she's in it?' Kate demanded.

'Climbed up,' Paul said morosely. 'Car nearly fell too. Had a quick look and got the hell out of there. If that car tips. . .'

'She's alive?'

Paul shook his head. 'Can't tell,' he said. 'She's certainly unconscious. I couldn't get in. Door's locked. I shone the torch in to see if there was anyone else.'

Kate bit her lip. 'OK, Paul,' she said at last. 'Give me a shove up.'

'You can't get up there,' Paul said, horrified. 'Damn thing'll tip on you. It damn near did on me.'

'It didn't, though,' Kate said firmly. 'And I'm lighter than you. Now, Paul.'

The big farmer stared at her and then shrugged. He knew as well as Kate that it might take half an hour to right the car, and meanwhile. . . 'You're sure?'

'I'm sure.'

Paul wasted no more time with words. He linked his hands, Kate stepped into them and he lifted. Kate heaved herself up, until she was balanced precariously on the side of the car. As she tried to find her balance the car moved slightly. Kate drew in her breath and waited, but the movement ceased.

'Hand me the lantern,' she ordered.

Taking the torch, she did a swift check of the car. As Paul had said, Dorrie was the only occupant. She was crumpled behind the wheel, lying at the base of the car.

Kate checked the door and grimaced. As Paul had said, it was firmly locked. The rear door was the same.

She stared down in indecision. She could see so little from where she was. If there was heavy bleeding, or airway obstruction. . . Or perhaps Dorrie was already dead.

She couldn't risk it.

'Find me a rock, Paul,' Kate ordered. 'A big one.'

'A rock. . .'

'I'm going to smash a window.'

'Glass'll fall on her,' Paul said morosely.

'I'll smash the rear side-window,' Kate said impatiently. 'Hurry, Paul.'

A minute later she had what she wanted. She wrapped her hands in her coat, raised the rock and smashed it down on to the glass. The glass fell away beneath her hands. Swiftly she broke away the jagged edges from the rim, until the frame was clear. It was impossible to get all the slivers out, but she hoped she had as much out as she could.

'Why on earth don't I wear trousers?' she muttered to herself. 'At least my tights are thick.' Grasping the edges of the window gingerly with her coat, she slowly lowered herself through the opening.

If she'd been a pound heavier she never would have made it. As it was, she had to hold her breath and squeeze. It was more difficult than she had imagined, lowering herself into the confined space in the dark. Her feet groped under her, trying to find a foothold. Finally her foot reached the other side of the car, grating on broken glass as it did. The rest of Kate's body slid inside.

It was disorientating, being inside a car lying at such

an angle. She tried to stand, but ended up crouched. For a moment she had to stay still, trying to work out the best way to gain access to the injured woman.

Finally she just leaned around, contorting her body to a crazy angle to reach round the seats. Dorrie was huddled into a corner, a limp and lifeless figure. Kate propped the lantern to one side and reached for the woman's pulse. As she did, Dorrie stirred and moaned.

'Easy, Dorrie,' Kate said gently. 'Don't move. You've crashed your car, but we're here to help.'

The woman stirred again, and then seemed to regain total consciousness in a rush. 'The children,' she gasped, jerking her head up. 'Alice. . .'

'Don't move your head,' Kate said sharply. 'It's important, Dorrie. Keep your head quite still.' Then, studiously casual, 'Were the children in the car with you?'

The woman's eyes came wide as if struggling to remember, and with remembrance came a rush of relief. 'No,' she breathed. 'They're with my sister. Oh, God, Kate, my chest. . .'

Kate allowed herself a moment's relief too. Dorrie knew her and was alert. Her chest. . . Dorrie was pinned hard behind the wheel. From the angle of the steering-wheel there would have to be broken ribs.

'Just keep quite still,' Kate said softly. 'The ambulance is coming, and the tow-truck. We'll have you out of here soon.' Her hands were still moving and suddenly they stopped. Her fingers had come in contact with blood. On the arm directly under Dorrie there was blood spurting from a wound Kate couldn't feel. She could feel the pressure of the blood, though. The window under Dorrie was smashed and Dorrie's arm had been driven into it. There must be a torn artery.

She could do nothing from the back seat. She couldn't even reach.

'Dorrie, I'm going to have to come around,' she said softly. 'You've cut your arm.'

'I know,' Dorrie told her. Her voice was amazingly matter-of-fact. 'I can feel the blood.'

'It'll be a squash,' Kate said. 'Hang on.'

Kate had been caving once as an adventurous teenager, and the experience came flooding back. Wriggling into impossible positions for crazy reasons. . . This wasn't a crazy reason, though. If that artery kept pumping. . .

'Kate?' A voice from outside the car made Kate jerk her head up. Richard. His voice was harsh and anxious. 'Kate, are you OK?' Then to someone outside, 'Why the hell did you let her get inside? The whole thing's going to go over. . .'

'Didn't have much choice,' Kate heard Paul say dourly. 'One of us had to and I'm sixteen stone.'

'Richard, I'm fine,' Kate called out. 'And Dorrie'll be OK too. Just as soon as I can get a tourniquet on.'

'I'll be fine even without a tourniquet,' Dorrie said defiantly. The adrenalin rush that had come with the regaining of consciousness was fading and Kate heard the signs of weakness from blood-loss beginning in her voice. 'I've plenty of blood.'

'You're telling me,' Kate said ruefully. 'But you're making an awful mess of the furnishings. I prefer to keep the container capped.'

Dorrie gave a rueful chuckle and then gasped. 'Oh, Kate. My chest.'

'It'll just be broken ribs,' Kate reassured her. 'Just try to relax and breathe slowly.' She had twisted herself into the front seat, bent almost double. Quickly she felt along Dorrie's arm, searching for pressure-points. Dorrie's weight was still heavily on the arm and it was difficult, but finally Kate found what she was looking for. She gripped hard and the spurting blood subsided. Kate gave a grunt of satisfaction.

'I've got the pressure-point,' she called to Richard. 'But I don't think. . . I can't put a tourniquet on the way the arm's lying. And Dorrie's wedged hard behind the steering-wheel. You'll have to get us both out together.'

'We're working on it,' Richard said grimly.

It was the most agonising few minutes Kate had ever known. Her head was below the rest of her body, and she had trouble fighting off the light-headedness that went with it. Dorrie lay silent, concentrating on her breathing.

'How's Ron?' Kate asked softly, as the moments stretched on. Dorrie's breathing was laboured and bubbly. Kate was starting to wonder whether she had punctured a lung.

'He's fine,' Dorrie whispered. 'The results of his tests came back today. His mole was cancer, but the rest of him seems clear.'

'That's great.'

'Yeah,' Dorrie said grimly. 'I've been that worried. And what do I do now but go and damn near kill myself. As if Ron hasn't enough to worry about.'

'It'll stop him having time to worry his stitches.' Kate tried to smile. Her body was cramping unbearably.

'Yeah.' They relapsed into silence.

Outside there were the sounds of men and vehicles. Kate heard the ambulance, and then the tow-truck and finally the unmistakable sounds of tractors.

'Kate, we're going to have to haul the car out of there,' Richard told her. 'We can't get access any other way.'

'You can't move the car,' Kate said grimly. 'Dorrie's arm is caught through the window.'

Silence while the men assimilated this. There was talking, silence and more talking.

'OK,' Richard said heavily. 'We've sent for the Jaws

of Life. They'll take about an hour. Do you think you can hang on for that long?'

Kate grimaced but she had expected no less. The Jaws of Life was a contraption designed to slice through car bodies. In this situation it was the only answer. Ideally every community should have one, but they were expensive and Corrook didn't have the population to support it.

'Can we hang on, Dorrie?' she said softly, and the older woman managed a chuckle.

'We're not going to sneak out on them, that's for sure,' she muttered.

Kate bit her lip. Dorrie's voice was laced with pain and exhaustion. 'Can you lower me some morphine?'

'Can you administer it in there?' Richard's voice was incredulous.

Kate moved awkwardly to face up to the broken window above her. 'If you load the syringe I'll give it my damnedest,' she said.

The time passed agonisingly slowly. Kate's fingers kept up their relentless pressure, releasing for only a few blessed moments each ten minutes to restore Dorrie's circulation. Dorrie drifted into an uneasy, drugged sleep.

For a while the men outside tried to talk to her, but Kate couldn't respond. It was all she could do to stay in the one position and keep pressure on Dorrie's arm. She had no energy for anything else.

'Kate?' Every few moments Richard would force her to speak, just a few words.

'I'm still here,' she said unsteadily.

'Good.' She could hear the smile in his voice and the thought of that smile jerked her into wakefulness. She had missed that smile so much over the last few days. 'It's good having you nicely parcelled,' he told her.

'Like having a can of beer and no can opener,' Kate managed, and the men outside laughed.

'Can opener's on its way, Doc.' Kate recognised the voice of the local tow-truck driver. 'Bloody big can opener too.'

It certainly was. Kate heard a siren screaming in the distance and closed her eyes with relief. Two minutes later the men outside were mobilised into action.

'We're coming through the roof,' Richard told her. 'Are you clear?'

'I can be,' Kate said, wriggling her body forward closer to Dorrie. Dorrie half woke and managed a smile.

'Getting cosy in here, Kate.' She closed her eyes again.

Three minutes later the roof of the car lifted away like the lid of a sardine can. Light shone into the car, augmenting Kate's fading lantern, and Richard's hands reached in to steady her.

'How on earth did you get yourself in that position?' he demanded incredulously.

'I wiggled,' Kate told him. 'And pushed. It's the only way I could reach Dorrie's arm.'

'OK,' Richard told her. 'We've a winch on the car body holding it steady. We'll lift it slightly while we pull Dorrie's arm free.'

'Can you do that?' Kate asked doubtfully.

'Not with you in there,' he told her. He moved to position his hand on the pressure-point on Dorrie's arm. 'OK, Kate. Out you go.' And strong arms lifted her clear.

Minutes later Dorrie also was being lifted from the wreck and carefully placed on a stretcher. Richard was inserting a saline drip almost before she was on the stretcher. Kate looked at her anxiously as she emerged. She was semi-conscious, but still able to try for a smile. 'Thank you all,' she whispered. 'Oh, Kate. . .'

Kate gripped the hand of her non-injured arm.

'You'll be fine,' she said softly. 'Dr Blair will look after you now.'

'Not you?'

Kate looked ruefully down at herself. She was filthy, smeared with blood from both Dorrie's injuries and the myriad scratches she had suffered crawling around the car. 'I think I'd better have a bath first,' she smiled. She was in no condition to operate as a doctor. Her limbs were screaming in protest from their unaccustomed position. A hot bath was the only answer. And fast.

'Come to the hospital, Kate,' Richard ordered. 'I want to check those cuts.' His attention, though, was almost solely on Dorrie. It had to be.

Kate shook her head. 'One of the men will drive me home,' she said firmly, and smiled thankfully as Paul stepped forward. She placed a hand down to pull her ripped skirt together as best she could. 'I'm in no condition to be seen in public for any longer.'

CHAPTER FOURTEEN

KATE ran a deep bath and lay in it for a very long time. Hours, she thought. As the water cooled she ran more hot, trying to soak away the blood and the grime and the bruising.

She was almost a hospital case herself, she decided, looking down at her naked body. There seemed nowhere that had escaped scratching.

Her little house was cold and barren. Everything was packed. There seemed no reason to get out of the bath.

Finally the supply of hot water was exhausted. Kate sighed with regret. She climbed carefully from the bath, her limbs protesting painfully, and rubbed herself dry. As she did she heard a car pull up outside. She would recognise the sound of that car anywhere. Richard.

By the time he knocked on the door, she had a bathrobe on and her damp curls wrapped turban-style in her towel. She opened the door a couple of inches and looked out.

'Yes. . .' She had meant her voice to sound business-like and brusque but it came out a squeak.

'You should have come down in the ambulance,' Richard said shortly. Kate could hardly see him on the dimly lit veranda. 'Some of those scratches looked deep.'

'I'll live.'

'I'm sure you will.' He hesitated. Kate kept the door firmly at two inches. 'Your fire's not lit,' he said.

'I'm going to bed.'

'With wet hair?'

'Richard. . .'

'Kate, don't be so bloody stupid.' Before she could

stop him the door had been wrenched open. Richard strode past her into the house. 'Honestly, girl. You haven't the brains you were born with. Let's get this damned fire lit.'

'There's no need to swear at me,' Kate said in a small voice.

'And there's no need to risk your life crawling round wrecked cars,' Richard said savagely. He had crossed to the hearth and was throwing kindling from the wood box into the grate. 'If that car had toppled. . .'

'It didn't,' Kate said evenly.

'Just as bloody well.'

'Will you stop swearing?'

Silence. Richard concentrated on the fire. Kate watched him for a moment and then made her way through to the kitchen and made coffee. She carried two mugs back, proud that she could make her hands operate without shaking. Richard was standing by the fire. He took the mug without speaking and placed it on the mantel.

'You drink yours,' he told her. 'I'll dry your hair.'

'But. . .'

'Just shut up and do as you're told,' he snapped. 'Sit.' He pointed to the armchair by the fire. For a moment Kate stared up at him. His eyes dared her to argue. She didn't have the strength. She sank into the armchair and Richard unwound her turban.

His anger slowly dissipated as he towelled her hair. Gradually the fire before them built up heat. Meg came through and leapt on to Kate's lap. The little cat gave her warmth in the same way as Richard's hands were warming her whole body. He towelled and towelled, and then found a brush from her bedroom and slowly brushed the tangled locks through and through, holding each section of hair up to the heat and letting it softly fall.

Kate leaned back, drifting, drifting, the tensions of

the night seeping out of her as Richard's hands worked their magic.

'You should be with Dorrie,' she said sleepily.

'I checked she was stable and then sent her to the city,' Richard said. 'We could have kept her here, but this way she'll be with Ron.'

'She's OK?'

'She's OK.'

Was it Kate's imagination or was he really a long way away? His voice was part of some lovely dreaming.

'Kate, what the hell were you doing risking your life like that?' Richard said suddenly, and his voice had changed. 'When I saw where you were. . .' His voice shook with remembrance and his hand stilled on her hair. 'I thought I could watch you walk away from the valley but. . .'

'But what?' Kate whispered.

Richard's hands stilled. 'Oh, God, Kate. . .'

Kate put a hand up and touched his still fingers. 'I love you, Richard,' she whispered from her dream world. 'I trust you with my life, Richard Blair. I wasn't frightened in that car, because I knew you would come.'

Richard knelt and took her face between his hands. 'If I thought you meant that. . .'

Kate shook her head. 'I can't give you more than that. . . I can't say more. . .'

He closed his eyes as if in pain. Kate's dreaming came to a sudden end. Richard's face closed and he stood. Taking his cup from the mantel, he took a sip and put it back as if it was foul. 'Words, my Kate,' he said harshly.

'Your coffee will be cold,' Kate said. Her voice no longer belonged to her, but the lovely feeling of warmth was dissipating. She had nothing left to fight with.

Richard put a finger down to touch her shoulder and she gave an involuntary shiver. 'It's you that's cold,' he said quietly.

'I was cold in the car,' Kate said. 'Freezing. I used my coat to hold back the glass and my clothes were ripped.'

'I saw.' Richard gave a tight smile. His eye caught sight of the mound of disreputable rags beside the chair. Lifting them up, his smile deepened. 'Thus endeth the skirt. It couldn't have happened to a better piece of clothing.'

'You can throw it on the fire,' Kate told him. 'All the clothes. They're ruined.'

Richard obliged with alacrity. The skirt was consigned to the flames. As he lifted the blouse, though, Richard hesitated as he felt something in the top pocket. His fingers searched and lifted out Miss Souter's cheque.

'You'd better not burn that,' Kate told him as she remembered its existence. 'In fact you can keep it.'

'Keep it?' He unfolded the cheque and then whistled as he saw its contents. 'What on earth. . .?'

'Miss Souter's legacy,' Kate told him. 'But if you'll give me a pen I'll sign it and you keep it. I decided in the car what I wanted done with it.'

Richard was still staring. 'What you want done. . .'

'I want you to have it,' Kate said softly. 'I've thought it all out. It's not mine. Miss Souter left it to me because she was lonely and isolated. The only thing I can do is ensure Corrook's elderly aren't as isolated in the future. I want you to put it towards units attached to the hospital—your dream of accommodation and social facilities for the elderly.'

'You want me. . .'

'You're good at dreaming,' Kate said gently. 'Use this money to build on to the dream.'

'You'd just sign the cheque tonight and give it to me. . .'

'Of course.'

There was a long, long silence. The fire crackled and

spluttered in the grate. Meg washed one paw with sleepy gentility and then nestled closer on to Kate's lap.

Finally Richard laid the cheque carefully on the mantel. He knelt before Kate and took her hands into his.

'You'd trust me that much, my Kate?'

'I'll always trust you,' she said softly. 'Always. If you'll let me. . .'

Meg was lifted carefully off Kate's lap. She cast Richard a disdainful look, but Richard didn't see. His eyes were all on Kate.

'Marry me, my Kate,' he said.

Kate's lovely dream was back as a swirling warmth of mist around her. Peace and happiness enfolded her. Here was the happy ending she had never dreamed of having. She put out a hand and touched the beloved face. 'My Richard,' she whispered. 'Oh, Richard. . .'

Then she was lifted from the chair to be held tightly in his arms. His lips met hers and her being was alight with love and light.

'My Kate,' he said slowly as their lips gently parted. 'My dream. . . My life. . .'

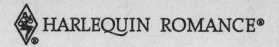

HARLEQUIN ROMANCE®

brings you

More Romances Celebrating Love, Families and Children!

Next month, look out for Emma Goldrick's new book,
Leonie's Luck, Harlequin Romance #3351
(a heart-warming story of romantic involvement between
Leonie Marshal and Charlie Wheeler, who marches
without warning—or permission—into her life!)

Charlie's nine-year-old daughter, Cecilia, who comes to
live with them—at Leonie's Aunt Agnes's invitation—is
somehow never far from what is going on and plays an
innocent part in bringing them together!

Available wherever Harlequin books are sold.

KIDS10

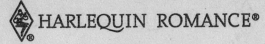

HARLEQUIN ROMANCE®

Last month we announced our Sealed with a Kiss series,
which starts in March. This is just to tell you about our
choice for that month which we know you will love!

Invitation to Love is the story of Heidi who needs
to make a living for herself, but when that livelihood
involves welcoming into her home handsome
Dillon Archer—the man she believes caused her
father's death—she's forced to swallow her pride!

Don't miss Harlequin Romance #3352
Invitation to Love
by Leigh Michaels

Available in March, wherever Harlequin books are sold.

SWAK-1

On the most romantic day of the year, capture the
thrill of falling in love all over again—with

Harlequin's

Bachelors

They're three sexy and *very single* men who run
very special personal ads to find the women of
their fantasies by Valentine's Day. These exciting,
passion-filled stories are written by bestselling
Harlequin authors.

Your Heart's Desire by Elise Title
Mr. Romance by Pamela Bauer
Sleepless in St. Louis by Tiffany White

Be sure not to miss Harlequin's Valentine Bachelors,
available in February wherever
Harlequin books are sold.

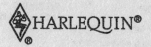

HARLEQUIN®

VB

Fifty red-blooded, white-hot, true-blue hunks
from every State in the Union!

Look for MEN MADE IN AMERICA! Written by some
of our most popular authors, these stories feature some
of the strongest, sexiest men, each from a different state
in the union!

Two titles available every month at your favorite
retail outlet.

In February, look for:

THE SECURITY MAN by Dixie Browning
(North Carolina)
A CLASS ACT by Kathleen Eagle (North Dakota)

In March, look for:

TOO NEAR THE FIRE by Lindsay McKenna (Ohio)
A TIME AND A SEASON by Curtiss Ann Matlock
(Oklahoma)

You won't be able to resist MEN MADE IN AMERICA!

If you missed your state or would like to order any other states that have already been published, send your name, address and zip or postal code, along with a check or money order (please do not send cash) in the U.S. for $3.59 plus 75¢ postage and handling for each book, and in Canada for $3.99 plus $1.00 postage and handling for each book, payable to Harlequin Reader Service, to:

In the U.S.

3010 Walden Avenue
P.O. Box 1369
Buffalo, NY 14269-1369

In Canada

P.O. Box 609
Fort Erie, Ontario
L2A 5X3

Please specify book title(s) with your order.
Canadian residents add applicable federal and provincial taxes.

MEN295